Born to Bl

A Victorian Romance

By Fran Connor

Published by Liot Literary

Other novels by Fran Connor

The Devil's Bridge

Someone to Watch Over Me

Sophia and the Fisherman

Passarinho and the Highlander

Her Man in Havana

Honourable Lies

Operation Hydra

The Genesis Project

The Alcazar Code

Dunkirk

Full many a flower is born to blush unseen and waste its fragrance on the desert air.

Jane Austen – Emma

ISBN: 9798642624357

Chapter One

Southampton, England 1840

Mary's tummy rumbled as she stood in the queue in the refectory for Monday night's supper. It was always soup and bread on Mondays: the smell of cabbage drifting along the line to her nostrils suggested the absence of meat, as usual. She preferred Sundays when beef and vegetables were served though not much of either. The bread and butter she had for breakfast seemed a long time ago, and she'd worked hard all day clearing the brambles at the back of Highfields House. She wiped her hands on her grey dress and winced at the cuts from the thorns. Mary wished they left the clearance to later in the year, she liked blackberries.

Thoughts of blackberries vanished as her eyes lowered to the flagstone floor when Mr Higgins, the Workhouse Porter, strode along the line with his brass topped walking cane that he didn't need for walking. He passed her. A yelp came from someone several places back. Mary waited for a minute before she looked up and then gave her brother George a poke in the back to make him move because as usual, he was daydreaming, and the queue had moved on.

Mary and George's turn came. Master and Matron stood behind the counter, their eyes running over each inmate to make sure no interlopers had sneaked in for a free meal.

Mary's short excursions from the Workhouse had shown her the poverty that existed outside. One of the older girls sloshed the soup into tin bowls. Another tore small chunks of bread and passed a piece to each resident.

They sat at the end of a wooden bench to eat their meal with wooden spoons in one hand and the other arm around their bowls to protect them from being snatched away. Five hollow faces on the other side of the trestle table did the same. The sound of three hundred scraping spoons filled the room.

Mary cast her eyes up when she heard a clanging bell to see Mr Higgins make his way through the refectory, the scraping stopped, not that there was anything left in the bowls to scrape.

With mealtime over Mary headed into the kitchen for her chore. "Ouch!" Cold dirty water in the zinc sink seeped into Mary's cuts. She stacked the tin bowls in columns of ten, upside down to dry. Job finished she wiped her hands on her dress and stepped outside into the courtyard to find George.

He sat on the ground leaning against the red brick edifice of the Southampton Workhouse. Mary threaded through the other inmates to her brother and sat down on the cold ground beside him.

"Will Dad come back for us?" he said playing with a black beetle in his hand.

"Gawd! Don't keep on so George. After Ma died, 'e could 'ave come home and looked after us, but that woman he left her for wouldn't let him. Please stop asking."

"Bastard!"

"Mind your language George. If Mr 'iggins catches you profaning, you'll get the brass."

"We've been here two years now Mary. I don't like it. Can't we run away?"

"George, you're eight and I'm ten. 'Ow long would we last out there with no money and no work? We need to stay here for another two years and then I can work as a scullery maid or in the kitchen at 'Ighfields 'Ouse. Johnny said his mother might employ me when I'm old enough. You keep on and on George and you know that upsets me."

"Johnny Sandes is a toff and you're sweet on him."

"I ain't sweet on 'im. He's kind. That's all."

"You're sweet on him. Mary loves Johnny. . . Mary loves Johnny."

"Stop it." Her sore fingers pinched his leg.

"Ow!"

"Stop it George. I'll be in trouble with your caterwauling and then I won't get a job with the Sandes. We'll 'ave to stay 'ere."

***

Mary lay on her back looking up at the board ceiling in the dim moonlight that filtered through the window. Could she really manage another two years in this place? She wasn't sure. Two years is a long time when you're ten. Someone coughed in one of the other eight beds. From another came sobbing. Whispers emanated from the one next to hers. She turned onto her side carefully so not to disturb George or the other two children sharing the bed. Something crawled over her neck and disappeared under the canvas bolster before she had chance to grab it.

After a bread-and-butter breakfast Mary collected a trowel from the store and set off with the work team for Highfields House to weed the vegetable garden ready for this year's crop. Mary liked weeding better than clearing brambles. If Johnny was around, that would be even better. Bertha and Margaret were on the gardening team. They wouldn't bully her if Johnny came into the vegetable garden. The school holidays were on though she hadn't seen him at church the previous day. George's ribbing about her being sweet on him touched a nerve because she was sweet on him even though he was so much older at thirteen.

Mr Bullington the head gardener met the work team at the gate in the walled garden.

"Good morning. Lovely day. Now let's see." He counted the children. "Seven. I'll put you into pairs with one on their own. Who wants to work on their own?"

Mary's hand shot up, but the haste was not necessary as nobody else put up theirs.

The gardener gave out jobs to everyone. Mary got the rhubarb patch to weed which was not the best place to be due to the amount of horse manure spread over the area.

Mr Bullington stepped over to the rhubarb patch with Mary. "Now, Mary, you see that plant there?" He pointed to a plant with oval leaves and purple bell-shaped flowers.

"Yes, sir."

"That's bella donna or deadly nightshade as it is often called. It's grown for medicinal purposes but it is highly poisonous if you don't know how to use it. So be very careful. Later in the year it will have black berries so do not touch them and do not eat them. Do you understand?"

"Yes, sir."

The only good thing about the patch was that weeds were few. The idea that she could be a gardener when she was old enough had often lingered in her mind. Being outdoors seemed a lot nicer than getting up at four in the morning to light the house fires if she was a scullery maid. How much a gardener earned she had no idea. Everyone knew the Master at the workhouse was paid for the work the children did. The children got nothing other than bed and board which seemed unfair to Mary. She wondered if it would be rude to ask Mr Bullington if it were possible for a twelve-year-old girl to train as a gardener. Her question would have to go unanswered for now as she couldn't see him in the garden.

Crouching rather than kneeling to stay out of the manure she pulled up a dandelion and then felt a shove in her back that sent her sprawling face first. A foot pressed down on her back forcing her further into the stinking mess.

"Oi! Leave her alone" Johnny's voice shrilled across the garden; it hadn't broken yet.

Mary managed to turn her head to see Bertha standing over her.

Bertha put her hands on her hips as Johnny came running towards the rhubarb patch.

"You horrible girl!" shouted Johnny pointing his finger at her.

She shrugged her shoulders, and as she wandered off to the far side of the walled garden called back, "Oh dear! I tripped."

"You're in more shit than Mary!" He bellowed after her as he helped Mary to her feet.

Tears ran down Mary's manure covered face as she tugged her sodden and stinking dress from clinging to her skin.

Mr Bullington came into the garden; his face took on an irritated expression. "What's going on Master John?"

"That girl," he pointed to Bertha now hoeing the onion patch as if butter wouldn't melt in her mouth. "She deliberately pushed Mary into the manure."

"I'll speak with Matron at the Workhouse; we can't have that. This child can't stay in that dress Master John. I suggest you take her into the house and have Mrs Tavistock see if she can wash her down and give her one of your sister's old dresses."

Mary stopped crying. She had never been inside Highfields House, the thought excited her, but she would prefer her first visit wasn't smelling of manure.

"C'mon," said Johnny keeping a few paces away from smelly Mary.

Chapter Two

Johnny took Mary to the back of the house and through a huge kitchen with a fire in the hearth and a black cooking rage on which boiled a chicken carcass.

Cook looked up from her baking table. "Good Lord Master John, take the smelly girl out of here."

They found Mrs Tavistock, an overweight grey-haired housekeeper with a kind face, in her office along the corridor from the kitchen.

"Oh my! What have we here?"

"Mary had an accident. Well, it wasn't an accident. One of the girls pushed her into the sh. . . into the manure."

"Oh dear. Well young lady you'd better come with me." Mrs Tavistock stood and bustled into the corridor with Mary following not too close behind.

Johnny waited in the kitchen.

Mary found herself in a room with white tiles, brass taps and the first bath she had ever seen. She shuffled from one foot to the other not knowing what she was expected to do.

"We're lucky because the boiler is on so there will be some hot water."

Mrs Tavistock turned a brass tap and to Mary's surprise water came out. At the Workhouse they pumped water into the basins, always cold water, even in winter when ice formed on the inside of the windows.

Mary watched the bath fill. Steam rose. She backed away. "Are you going to boil me?"

"No, don't be silly. I'll put some cold water in before you get in. Now get out of those stinky clothes."

Mary wasn't sure about undressing in front of this lady even if she had a kind face

"Come on girl! We haven't got all day. Chop chop!!

Mary slipped out of her dress and stood in her grey drawers that once may have been white. Mrs Tavistock turned off one tap and turned another on. After a few minutes, the housekeeper put her elbow in the water, nodded and turned off the water.

"All right. Pop yourself in. I'll go and find you something to wear."

Mary stood alone in the bathroom staring at the water in the bath unsure sure if she should get in. Her hand swirled the water, it felt warm. She slipped off her drawers and climbed into the bath when she heard footsteps in the corridor.

Mrs Tavistock came in carrying a blue dress and a pair of white drawers. "Here we are. These belong to Miss Susan, but she's outgrown them. Her mother never throws anything away, quite rightly. How's the bath?"

Mary nodded. "It feels good Ma'am."

"Splendid. Now let's get you scrubbed down." She reached into a cupboard and came out with a bar of white soap.

Mary liked the smell of it. The soap in the Workhouse was brown and made her skin sore. Carbolic she heard one of the older girls call it.

Mrs Tavistock handed her a flannel and the soap. "Now wash yourself all over and then we'll do your hair."

Mary scrubbed herself with the nice smelling soap while Mrs Tavistock fussed around in a cupboard looking for something. She came out with an enamel jug and a blue towel. The clear bathwater turned to grey. Mary thought of the procedure at the Workhouse where the ablutions consisted of washing face and hands every morning and evening and once a week a wash all over with the carbolic

The housekeeper filled the jug with hot water and added some cold. "Now the hair." She poured the water over Mary's head and rubbed the soap into her hair with a brisk action until it lathered up and ran down into her eyes.

"Yow!" hollered Mary.

"Sorry." She poured more water over Mary's head. "Splendid. Hop out and wrap yourself in this towel."

Mary climbed out and engulfed herself in the towel.

"Splendid. You're dry. Put these on and I'll see you in the kitchen." She left Mary to dress.

Mary pulled on the drawers and then the blue dress. Her mouth fell wide open when she saw her reflection in a mirror on the wall. Such a dress she had never even touched and to be wearing it made her heart sing. A look of disappointment passed over her face when she saw the scruffy black ankle boots that were her only footwear. Unsure of what to do with her grey dress she rolled it into a bundle with her drawers inside and left it in the corner.

A quick peek out into the corridor and then she set off for the kitchen at a pace where Mrs Tavistock, the cook, and Johnny sat at the table.

"My you look a picture," said Mrs Tavistock.

"And you don't smell as bad," laughed Johnny.

Mary pulled her tongue out at him and then quickly pulled it back in remembering where she was.

"Well, lassie, I expect after your excitement you could do with something to eat," said Cook in an accent that Mary recognised as Scottish because one of the Workhouse girls came from up there.

Cook ladled out a bowl of chicken soup and cut a large piece of bread. "Get that inside you and you'll feel better."

Mary sat at the table and ate the chicken soup. She hadn't tasted anything so good since her mother died.

"When should I bring the dress back, Ma'am?"

"I'll ask Mrs Sandes if you can keep it. Finish your soup."

Mrs Tavistock smiled and left Mary with Johnny and Cook. She finished the soup and bread slowly so she could enjoy every mouthful.

"That girl who pushed you into the. . . into the manure, is she always nasty?" said Johnny.

Mary cast her eyes down to the table. "Yes, Master Johnny. Her and her friend Margaret are always picking on us younger girls."

Cook shook her head, "It's hard enough for the bairns in that place without bullying."

Two sets of footsteps came along the corridor. Mrs Tavistock followed an elegant lady in a powder blue dress, a mob cap, and a worried expression. Mary had seen Mrs

Sandes only at a distance but she recognised her, stood, and made a curtsey.

"Hmmm. That was one of Susan's favourite dresses," said Mrs Sandes. "But she grew out of it a long time ago. It's on the large size for you but I expect you will grow into it. Little girl, what is your name?"

"Mary, Ma'am."

"Mary what?"

"Mary Dunsford, Ma'am."

"All right, Mary Dunsford, you may keep the dress."

"Thank you, Ma'am." She curtseyed again.

Mary felt a rush of joy run through her whole body. She had a real dress. Not even when her mother was alive did she have something as fine as this to wear. What a wonderful day. A new dress and a bowl of delicious soup. She didn't want to take her grey dress with her but Mrs Tavistock insisted.

***

Mary couldn't help beaming a huge smile when she joined the garden detail for the walk back to the Workhouse. She could see jealousy all over Bertha's face and her partner in crime, Margaret, looked equally miffed.

"You ain't keeping that dress," hissed Bertha.

"Oh, but yes I am. And you can't do anything about it!" said a defiant Mary.

Matron stood at the Workhouse entrance as the team came back. "Mary Dunsford, what do you think you are doing wearing that? Where did you get it?"

"She stole it Miss," said Bertha.

"What?"

"I didn't steal it Miss. Bertha pushed me into the sh. . . the manure and Master John got the 'ousekeeper at 'Ighfields 'Ouse to give me a bath and a clean dress. Mrs Sandes said I can keep the dress."

"No, you can't," said Matron with a look that brooked no argument. "It will create two of the seven deadly sins, envy and pride, and we cannot tolerate that in this establishment. I take it that bundle is your allotted dress. Take it to the laundry and wash it. And I'll bring you a Workhouse dress to wear until yours is dry. Now go." She pointed along the corridor.

With her feet dragging, Mary headed for the laundry.

***

Mary sat on her the bed she shared with her brother and two of the other younger children. The Workhouse dress itched. She feared it had fleas.

Bertha and Margaret came in laughing. Bertha pointed at Mary. "Told you that you couldn't keep the dress. Serves you right for trying to be above your station thinking Johnny Sandes gives a fig about you."

Mary stood. She felt as if an ice flow ran through her blood as Bertha came and stuck her face in front of her. Her fingers tingled. She balled her fist and drove it hard into Bertha's face knocking her backwards onto the bed and then she jumped on her with her knees one each side of the thirteen-year old's chest and punched her in the face again.

An arm went round her neck. Margaret dragged her backwards off Bertha and held her in the crook of her elbow across her throat choking her.

One day when it rained and the work in the garden had to stop while everyone took shelter, Mary had managed to sneak off and play with Johnny. He taught her a throw to get out of such a hold he learned at school. It consisted of quickly bending the knees bringing the assailant's pelvis over the shoulder then straightening up shoving the attacker over the shoulder to land on their back.

She tried this move in her current predicament and suddenly Margaret sailed through the air to land on her back with a thud and a scream.

Mary turned back to Bertha who scrabbled off the bed away from her. Margaret ran from the room.

Minutes later Matron came rushing in with Mr Higgins. He carried his brass topped walking cane. Margaret came in behind the porter.

Bertha sat on the floor, crying as she held her hand to her bloody nose.

"She hit Bertha for no reason, Ma'am," lied Margaret.

"You dreadful girl! Three days solitary on bread and water. Take her to the cellar Mr

Higgins."

Mary stood erect and marched out of the room with her head held high. For two years Bertha and Margaret had bullied her. They wouldn't do that again.

Chapter Three

Southampton, England 1842

Mary sat on the hospital pauper's ward bed and wiped her brother's forehead with a damp cloth. His breath laboured.

"Am I dying, Mary?"

"You'll be right as sixpence in a few days, George. Mark my words." But she didn't believe any of it. He wouldn't be the first boy to die from inhaling soot in the chimneys. Mary pleaded with the Master not to apprentice him to the chimney sweep. It was common knowledge that the Master received money for loaning out children and the older inmates to work on farms, estates, factories and in the chimneys. But nobody would tell on them; too many people made money by employing the cheap labour from the Workhouse. The Master's hard face when he refused to let George do something other than the chimneys would not leave her thoughts.

George coughed. Mary wiped away the blood and made a vow to herself and God that she would see the Master and Matron held responsible for their money grabbing schemes.

George coughed again and this time couldn't stop. Mary tried to hold him but his whole body racked and then suddenly he went limp. Mary looked into his face. His eyes glazed and his breathing stopped.

Mary let out a howl.

***

At the back of St Mary's churchyard where they buried the paupers, Mary stood beside a hole in the ground and looked down on the wooden box that held her brother. Johnny Sandes stood beside her. A stocky man with a shovel filled in the hole while Mary watched.

There would be no stone. Just a wooden square with a number on.

"He wouldn't need to go up chimneys if could get a job. He kept asking me to run away. I wouldn't. It's my fault he died."

"No, Mary. It isn't your fault."

Mary turned from the grave and headed towards the road with Johnny beside her. "Did you ask your mother if she would take me on as a scullery maid or gardener or anything?"

"I did, Mary. I didn't want to say anything yet. Not until you get over this though I know it is something that you won't get over soon, if ever. Mary, my mother was willing to take you on as a maid and train you to be a Lady's maid but the Master at the Workhouse spoke to my father and I'm so sorry but my father said you are not to be employed at Highfields House. I have no idea why."

Mary stopped and looked at him. "I know. I made a complaint to the Trustees of the Workhouse. I said the Master and Matron received payment for work done by the children. They called me a liar. I think the Master threatened your father because he 'ad a lot of work done by the children and the older inmates at a cost much less than employing local tradesmen. They don't want me in this area in case I manage to get someone in authority to believe me."

"If that is true then I hate my father."

"Don't 'ate, Johnny. Don't 'ate. Get even but don't 'ate."

"What will you do?"

"The Master found me a position somewhere. I don't know where it is other than in the direction of Portsmouth. 'Ousemaid. It'll be far enough away to stop me being a nuisance."

"Are you going to take it?"

"If I can't work at 'Ighfields, I'll have to take it or stay at the Workhouse or live on the street and I think something could 'appen to me if I stay. Without references I'll struggle to get work anywhere else."

"Really? Oh my God, I had no idea."

"Johnny, I don't think I'm gonna to see you again after today. You're off back to Eton on Monday and I'll be going to my new work."

"I'll miss you Mary."

"I'll miss you too Johnny. You've been kind to me. You didn't need to be, but you were, and I'll never forget you."

Johnny held out his hand for Mary to shake it. She shook her head instead and kissed him on the cheek.

Chapter Four

Mary gazed in awe at the huge grey stone building at the
end of a long drive lined with trees the names of which
she did not know. Two massive iron gates on stone pillars
topped with bronze pineapples barred the entrance. They
didn't have pineapples on the menu at the Workhouse so
she didn't know what these odd shapes represented.

Higgins, the Workhouse Porter, tapped the chestnut mare
on the rump with his whip. The cart carried on past the
gates and along the road until they came to a gravel track
running at ninety degrees to the road bounded by
brambles. Mary knew brambles. Off to her left she could
see farmland disappearing into the distance and on her
right the long wall that contained Hartford House. Mary
would not be arriving at the front entrance. She knew the
transport arrangement to get her there was to ensure that
she did arrive; with no alternative she had given in and
accepted the post. Ordinarily she expected girls being sent
to their first employment position had to make their own
way. Mary wore the transport like a badge of pride. She
rattled the Master and Matron so much they sent her under
guard. Maybe she hadn't finished the job for George's
memory but she'd done as much as she could though the
guilt still haunted her when she lay awake at night.

An open gate in the wall gave access to a cobbled stable
yard. Higgins pulled the mare up. "Here you are. Behave
yourself you little bitch."

Mary climbed down from the cart. Higgins threw down her blanket wrapped bundle that held her worldly belongings; a second grey dress and a spare pair of drawers. The mare clip clopped out through the gate leaving Mary standing on the cobbles with butterflies in her tummy and her tongue stuck out at the disappearing porter.

"Good day. You the new housemaid?" said a voice behind her making her jump.

She turned to see a man in a pair of brown trousers with string around each leg just below the knee and a red neckerchief above his collarless grey shirt.

"Yes, sir. Do you know which way I should go in?"

"Come with me," said the man with a smile. "I'm Andy. I'm one of the stable hands. Just a word of warning, the Mistress Lady Glendenning is a good woman, the butler Mr Stevens is a good man, the housekeeper Mrs Jones is a nice person and the Master, Sir Edward Glendenning is a devil and no mistake so watch your step with him."

"Thank you. Do I call you Mr Andy?"

"No, you call me Andy. What's your name?"

"Mary."

"Welcome to Hartford House, Mary." He pushed open a wooden door and stepped inside.

Mary picked up her bundle and followed him along a spotlessly clean corridor with landscape paintings on the wall. Her ankle boots made a clicking sound on the flagstone floor. A scent of lavender hung in the air from sprigs on the windowsills.

"Better get the metal off those boots or a new pair. Master won't like the noise," said Andy as they came to a door on which he knocked with a grubby hand.

"Come in," came the reply from inside.

Andy nodded at the door, turned, and walked away.

Mary pressed the door handle down and pushed it gently open. A middle-aged woman with a pair of spectacles on the end of her nose sat writing at a desk in the windowless room.

"And who be you?" said the woman.

"I'm Mary Dunsford, Ma'am. The new 'Ousemaid."

"Housemaid, not 'Ousemaid. Good. I'm Mrs Jones the housekeeper and you are to call me Mrs Jones not Ma'am. About names, you will call the mistress Milady and the master, sir. The butler is Mr Stevens and you'll get to know all the other staff in due course. Now is that all your baggage?"

Mary felt a tinge of shame as she glanced at her bundle and nodded.

"We don't nod here or shake our heads. We say yes or no."

"Yes, Ma'am. . . I mean Mrs Jones." *No nodding and no shaking of head. Sound your aitches. This is gonna be 'ard. . . h...hard.*

"Relax girl. I'm not going to bite you. First, we need to find you some decent clothes to wear. We can't have you working in the house dressed like a scarecrow. Come with me."

Mrs Jones took Mary to a room along the corridor that held sheets, blankets, towels, white aprons, black dresses, and white caps. A not unpleasant smell of fresh laundry pervaded the storeroom. The contrast with the smelly laundry at the Workhouse could not have been greater.

The housekeeper looked Mary over, selected two black dresses, two aprons and two caps and handed them to the recruit. "Now follow me."

They climbed a wooden staircase up three floors to the attic with Mary's ankle boots making a clicking sound on each step.

Halfway up the stairs Mrs Jones turned to Mary. "Oh dear. We can't have that. I'll see if Joe, the master's valet can obtain some more suitable footwear for you."

Sound your aitches, no nodding or shaking of heads and no noise from boots. Blimey!

The stairs opened out to a corridor that ran the length of the house with windows at each end. Mrs Jones stopped at the fourth door on the right from the staircase, pushed it open and waved Mary to enter.

Mary stepped into the room and saw it had a sloping roof which came down to a window where the height, she reckoned, would just about allow her to look out without ducking. A single iron bedstead with a mattress, pillow, sheets, and quilt lay with the head against the external wall. A wardrobe and a washstand that held a large pottery jug and basin were the only other items in the room. She looked at the bed and tried to hold back a grimace, but it showed on her face.

"What's wrong?" said Mrs Jones.

"Er. . . 'ow… how many of us sleep in the bed Mrs Jones because it isn't very wide."

Mrs Jones let out a laugh and then stopped. "I'm sorry. It isn't funny after what I suspect you were used to. This room, this bed is for your use only."

Mary's mouth fell open. "Blimey! For me? I am to stay in this room on my own?"

"Yes, Mary. And we don't say blimey."

Mary added another word to her list of things not to do or say but she couldn't keep the beaming smile from her face.

"Now get changed and come down when you're ready. You'll start your duties tomorrow morning so today you can get to know the layout of the house and the other staff.

And we'll see if we can get you some shoes."

Mrs Jones left Mary in the room. She sat on the bed and stared in amazement at the wardrobe and then walked over to the window. She had a view across to the impressive main entrance gates.

"Oh my! If only the Master and Mistress, Bertha and Margaret could see me now!" she said out loud.

***

Mary, dressed in a long black dress, white apron and mob cap followed Mrs Jones into a wide entrance hall with a crystal chandelier, a boar's head on a wall, a glass case with a stuffed salmon and a carved wooden staircase. Her heels clicked across the mosaic floor.

"Joe is soling a pair of shoes for you. Try to walk on your toes when on the hard floors until they are ready," said Mrs Jones stopping at a double door with a gilt pattern and porcelain handles. "Call her Milady and curtsey when we go in."

Mrs Jones knocked on the door.

A woman's voice from inside replied. "Come."

Mrs Jones turned the porcelain handle and pushed open the door ushering Mary to enter before her.

Mary stepped into the room. *Blimey*! A grand piano stood next to French doors, an Adams fireplace with unlit logs had a portrait of an elegant woman over the mantelpiece and a suite of red upholstered sofa and two armchairs gave the room a comfortable ambience though Mary was feeling anything but comfortable for this first interview with her new employer. Dappled sunlight filtered through tall bushes outside to shadow dance on the mullioned windowpanes.

Lady Elizabeth sat in one of the armchairs. "This is Mary? You work hard and we will see to it that you are cared for. A happy household makes for an efficient household and the other way around too."

"Thank you, Milady," said Mary with a curtsey trying to digest what Lady Elizabeth said. She noticed the resemblance of the woman in the chair to the woman in the portrait.

"Yes, that's me," said Lady Elizabeth with a smile. "And that one over there," she pointed to a woman's portrait on the opposite wall. "That's my mother. This estate has been in my family for three hundred years. Welcome."

Mary hadn't much education but was bright enough to guess that Lady Elizabeth's

husband had married well.

The kindness of the lady surprised Mary. Andy the stable groom said she was good but

Mary hadn't expected such a warm greeting. She decided immediately that she liked Lady Elizabeth and would do all she could to make her like her back.

***

Mary started work at four in the morning and finished at six in the evening with half an hour break for lunch for the first two years but her diligence was rewarded by Mrs Jones and she found herself promoted to housemaid at the age of fourteen.

The hours changed to eight in the morning to six in the evening. This new post gave her the run of the whole house as she was expected to clean all the rooms except the bedrooms.

That role was for the chambermaids who were another level higher than her.

After two years as housemaid Mary felt comfortable and happy doing her job that gave her a roof over her head, food in her belly and a little money in her pocket. Though she tried to hold on to the memory of George, he had begun to fade.

***

On a morning with the sun shining through the windows, sixteen-year-old Mary knelt on the wooden floor in a corridor on the upper floor rubbing her polish into the boards and daydreaming. Years had passed since she saw Johnny Sandes but his face kept popping up in her mind. She wondered what he was doing now. Perhaps he had gone to university or maybe joined the army or navy.

Something touched her skirt making her jump as a hand slid up her leg. The shock caused her to knock over her tin of polish and swing around to see Sir Edward bending down to her. She scurried forward, stood up and turned to face him. What to say, she had no idea. Some of the staff spoke about his wandering hands but this was the first time he had touched her. Fear began to creep through her tummy. If she didn't play this right, she could be dismissed but she couldn't let him have his way with her. No, that would be a step too far.

The voices of Lady Elizabeth and Mrs Jones coming up the stairs made him step back.

"Mention this and you will be out of a job." Sir Edward turned and marched off down the corridor.

"Good morning, Mary," said Lady Elizabeth as she passed Mary still standing with a polishing rag in her hand.

"Come on girl, get on with it," said Mrs Jones.

***

Mary sat at the kitchen table polishing brass candlesticks. Three weeks had passed since the incident with Sir Edward and since then, he had not tried anything again mainly because she managed to stay out of his way.

Lady Elizabeth came in. In her rush to get to her feet and curtsey, Mary dropped a candlestick which bounced on the flagstone floor. "Sorry Milady." Mary bent down to pick it up and saw that it had a dent in the base.

"Don't worry about that, Mary. I want you to learn carriage handling. I've asked Andy to show you."

"Oh!"

"Yes, I know. It's a role usually carried out by a man but I have my reasons. Also, I will need a lady's maid when

Jane leaves at the end of summer to marry. I would like you to replace her. Are you interested in that post?"

"Indeed, I am Milady. I thank you." Mary bobbed a curtsey.

"I want you to work with Jane to learn what is required. I know you can read and write but I think your education could do with expanding so I have arranged for Mr Stevens to give you lessons three mornings per week in arithmetic, English and history and most important, elocution."

Mary's mouth fell open with surprise. If only the Master and Mistress at the workhouse could see her now. They sent her to this estate to get her out of the way so she couldn't damage their financial shenanigans and they would never have expected her to do so well.

Apart from Sir Edward, Hartford House was a sanctuary.

***

Andy strapped the two-seater carriage harness to a chestnut mare while Mary watched.

"You see how it's done?"

"Yes, Andy."

"Good, now get up there and we'll go for a ride."

Andy helped Mary into the two wheeled carriage with a bench seat and cover but no sides and off they went through the Hampshire countryside. By the time they travelled three miles Mary had the hang of it.

After two more excursions, while Mary unhitched the horse watched by Andy, Lady Elizabeth glided across the stable yard in her usual elegant manner.

"Ah, Andy. Is you pupil now ready to take charge of the carriage and drive me?"

"She is, indeed, Milady. A natural." He touched his forehead with a crooked forefinger.

"Splendid."

***

The lessons with Mr Stevens, the instructions from Jane on how to be a lady's maid and with the added competence of carriage driver, at the tender age of sixteen Mary was a well-rounded asset to the Hartford Estate. Sir Edward hadn't tried anything with her since that one incident. Mary was aware that he spent some nights in the next room to hers with Brenda a buxom twenty-year old chambermaid. The noises coming from there left her in no doubts what was happening. Though common knowledge, nobody dared raise it or talk about it, not even Brenda such was the power of Sir Edward to keep people quiet for fear of losing their jobs.

When Mary had a spare few minutes, she would wander around the far part of the garden away from the formal part. She enjoyed listening to the birds and looking at the flowers. It reminded her of Johnny and the time they used to spend playing in his garden.

Perhaps he had married a well-connected young lady.

In a dip she saw a clump of bella donna growing. *That ought to be cut down, it's dangerous.* It reminded her of the day Bertha pushed her into the rhubarb. Bertha never bothered her again after the fight in the Workhouse. A smile crept across her face.

The first day of September was Mary's first day as lady's maid on her own. Jane had left the day before to travel to Basingstoke where her family lived and where she would marry.

"Good morning, Mary," said Lady Elizabeth as Mary knocked and entered the bedroom. "Lay out my Monday day clothes and an extra chemise and two pairs of drawers please."

Mary laid out the required items and wondered why her mistress wanted a change of underwear laid out.

"We're going for a ride. It's a beautiful day. Pack an extra pair of drawers and chemise

for yourself. Also take two large towels from the laundry. And ask Cook for a packed lunch."

After preparing Lady Elizabeth for her day, Mary took the backstairs up to her room and packed a spare pair of drawers and chemise in her canvas bag. What was going on, she had no idea but it intrigued her. On her way down she took two towels from the laundry cupboard.

"Where are you going with those?" said Mrs Jones coming around the corner.

"I have no idea. Milady told me to bring two towels, we're going for a ride. That's all I know."

"Hmmm." Mrs Jones smiled. "Can you swim?"

"No."

"Hmmm. Should be interesting."

***

Mary, with Lady Elizabeth beside her, urged the horse onwards following directions given by her mistress. Though she had no time piece with her, Mary could tell by the high sun that noon approached just before they went into the shade of a wood by the shore.

"Stop here," instructed Lady Elizabeth.

Mary climbed down and hitched the horse to a branch before helping her mistress from the carriage. Through the trees Mary could see and hear waves lapping on the pebble beach of a small cove.

"We're going for a swim, Mary. It's a very naughty thing to do in a place like this but it's private. We should use bathing machines and enter the water from them so nobody can see all of us. But I don't give a fig. Come on." Lady Elizabeth began to unbutton her dress.

"Come on Mary!"

"I can't swim, Milady."

"How do you know?"

"I beg your pardon, Milady. What do you mean? I've never been swimming."

"Exactly. You're a fast learner. Come on. Spit spot! Get undressed."

Mary's fingers fumbled as she undressed.

When both were down to their drawers and chemises, Lady Elizabeth said. "Race you!" She ran out of the wood squealing with a mixture of pain and delight as her bare feet touched the beach.

Mary followed looking right left and behind as she crossed the beach lifting each foot carefully as she went. The thought that Lady Elizabeth had lost her mind crossed hers.

With a splash, her mistress, now a few yards out in the water dived and swam around in a circle to face back to Mary who stood up to her ankles in the water. "Come on in!"

"I can't swim, Ma'am."

Lady Elizabeth swam towards Mary and then stood and walked the rest of the way through the waves. "It's easier to swim in the sea than a lake because of the salt water. It makes you more buoyant. Now come with me and you will be fine." She took Mary by the hand and led her deeper into the water.

The shock of cold water on her tummy took Mary's breath away.

"Now lower yourself into the water."

Mary would rather get back to the shore and dressed but Lady Elizabeth seemed intent on teaching her to swim.

After an hour Mary's teeth chattered and she felt as if she had drunk several pints of seawater but much to her joy, she found herself swimming alongside her mistress though her strokes lacked finesse.

Back on shore they dried themselves down, dressed and tucked into the packed lunch.

"Well Mary, did you enjoy that?"

"I did, Milady."

"Good. Subject to the weather and other commitments we will do this every Monday."

"Yes, Milady."

"Mary, please answer this question. Nothing will happen to you if you answer me truthfully." Lady Elizabeth washed down a bite of sandwich with a glass of lemonade.

Mary could see her face had gone from the happy smiles and laughter in the sea to one of seriousness. She wondered what was coming and felt her appetite disappear even though the cold water and exercise had burned up a lot of energy.

"Yes, Milady."

"Has my husband made any indecent approaches to you?"

There it was. She knew he spent a lot of his time away from the house and hadn't bothered her since that one time when she was polishing the floor. At home he'd moved on from Brenda and turned his attention to Joyce one of the stable girls via Barbara, a housemaid. Mary desperately wished Mrs Jones would do something but she always acted as if she didn't know what was going on.

"Milady. . . he has not made any advances towards me. Well, I must tell the truth. Not since he put his hand up my skirt when I was polishing the floor last year. He was disturbed from doing anything else with you and Mrs Jones' arrival."

"Hmmm. Then you are fortunate that is all. I'm so sorry you had to suffer such an indignity. Are you aware of any advances he has made towards other members of staff?"

The last thing Mary wanted was to be drawn into a domestic contest between Lady Elizabeth and Sir Edward but she was on the spot.

"Milady, do you really want to know?" Mary asked in a tone that belied her young years, more in the manner of a good friend cautioning her that she may not want to know the truth.

"Yes, Mary, I do need to know."

"Will the girls get into trouble?"

"No, Mary. I am aware of the power my husband wields. I shall ensure they are protected."

"Milady, I know he was intimate against their wishes with Brenda, Barbara and Joyce. There may have been others that I am unaware of."

"Thank you for your candour, Mary. Do not worry. Neither you nor they will come to any harm. We live in a time when a wife has truly little power. I am unable to divorce my husband without an Act of Parliament and his dalliance with staff would not be considered grounds. The laws would not prosecute him for what he has done with the girls because that is the way it is. But thank you for the information and I may use it against him if I have the opportunity."

Chapter Five

Hamble, England 1849

Mary pushed the door open with her foot and carried a
tray of beef broth into Lady Elizabeth's bedroom: she
placed it on the bedside table. The pallor of the woman's
skin stood witness to the fact that the end was near. Lady
Elizabeth had done so much for Mary in the seven years
she had worked at Hartford House, the thought of losing
her guiding light cut deep into her.

"Can I help you with something to eat, Milady?"

The Mistress coughed, a look of pain and fear crossed the
gentlewoman's face but with a hoarse voice she managed
to say. "Yes, please."

Mary plumped the pillows and helped her to sit up.
Another coughing fit ensued. When she stopped, Mary
lifted the bowl of soup and a spoon. With each mouthful,
she wiped her mistress's mouth with a napkin.

With half the soup gone, Lady Elizabeth raised her hand.
"That's enough thank you." Mary could see she was
exhausted.

A gentle knock on the door heralded a visitor which Mary
knew must be either the doctor or Sir Edward. Sir Edward
had restricted all visitors except himself, the doctor and
Mary. He only allowed Mary, in her opinion, because

Lady Elizabeth needed a lady's maid to see to her personal needs.

Doctor Kilbride, a portly gentleman with grey hair, a port nose and mutton chop whiskers entered carrying his leather medical bag. "Good day Lady Elizabeth."

She coughed a response.

Mary moved to the window and gazed out to give some privacy to the examination.

The examination over, the doctor headed for the door. "I shall return tomorrow. Try to rest."

Mary gritted her teeth. Try to rest was about the stupidest thing the stupid doctor could say, in her opinion. She had taken him aside when her mistress fell ill and asked if she had been poisoned. He claimed it was a fever and not poisoning but she didn't believe him and when she looked into his eyes, she could see he didn't believe it either. Belladonna grew in the grounds.

Her suspicions were aroused when Sir Edward sent her out of the drawing room when an argument developed after Lady Elizabeth challenged her husband over his treatment of the servant girls. Three days later she was taken ill and had been in bed for a week.

The door opened and in marched Sir Edward Glendenning in a riding jacket and boots.

"How are you today, dear?" he inquired with the sincerity of a politician on the run up to polling day.

Lady Elizabeth mumbled.

Mary picked up the tray with the bowl of soup.

"Before you go Mary, and while Sir Edward is here," she coughed again. "Please, get Mrs Jones and one of the chambermaids to come in. Then go into my jewellery box, you know where it is." She began coughing uncontrollably. Mary put the tray down, put her arm around her mistress and lowered her onto her side.

"I've expressly forbidden any visitors, Elizabeth. It is for your own good. You need to rest."

Sir Edward stood with a dark expression on a face that Mary had come to fear.

When Lady Elizabeth recovered enough to speak again, she said, "From the jewellery box take the diamond earrings, you know, the ones I wore when Queen Victoria visited. You are to have them with my grateful thanks for everything you have done for me while I have been ill and before then."

"Now wait a minute, Elizabeth. You can't go giving diamond earrings to a maid."

"They are my earrings and I shall do with them what I wish."

"Hmmm," said Sir Edward.

"Go on Mary. Fetch the earrings, Mrs Jones and one of the other servants. I need them as witnesses."

"What the devil! Elizabeth, what do you think you are doing?"

"I know what I am doing, Edward. I'm making sure that I leave Mary something for I know you would do your best to ensure nobody but you received anything. You will have the house and the grounds and all that my family have amassed over the centuries, be satisfied with that when I am gone."

Mary shuffled on her feet. Sir Edward was a dangerous man to cross. Once Lady Elizabeth was gone, she was nervous that he may make physical moves towards her. There would be no defence. Though Mrs Jones and Mr Stevens were supportive and respectable, they would not intervene because that would cost them their jobs and when someone was dismissed from service finding another position of an equal standing was almost impossible.

"Please, fetch the earrings and the others," said Lady Elizabeth with a cough.

Mary opened a door in a black and gold lacquered Japanese cabinet that held several jewellery boxes, lifted a walnut box, and carried it over to the bedside.

"Now fetch Mrs Jones and one other."

Mary found Mrs Jones in the kitchen and Brenda in the laundry room folding sheets.

She brought them to Lady Elizabeth's bedroom.

"Thank you for coming, Mrs Jones, Brenda. I want you to. . . I want you to stand witness for me."

"Humph," muttered Sir Edward. He sat on a chair.

Mary could feel his eyes boring into her.

With a wince and a painful expression Lady Elizabeth lifted the jewellery box lid. The top section of the box held pearl, silver, and gold earrings. She then lifted the cantilevered top to reveal amber, ruby and diamond earrings below and took two diamond earrings and handed them to Mary. "These are for you. You may want to sell them, or you may want to keep them. Whatever you do with them it is your choice. You see Edward, I have given these earrings to Mary and you are my witness should anyone doubt that. Mrs Jones, Brenda, you are also witnessing. I'm afraid I'm too ill to change my Will but there is something in it for all the staff."

"Thank you, Milady," said Mary.

Brenda and Mrs Jones curtsied and hurried out of the door.

***

Mary stood with Mrs Jones at the back of the graveside mourners in St Andrew's churchyard. The vicar intoned but Mary's thoughts were cast back to another graveyard where her brother lay. A tear escaped. Mrs Jones put her arm around her. The budding branches of an oak tree swayed in a cold breeze. At the far side of the cemetery a pile of last Autumn's leaves smouldered adding an acrid taste to the air.

The vicar finished his intoning which the servants under the direction of Mr Stevens took as the signal to board a horse drawn omnibus arranged specially by the butler to take them to the church and the internment and afterwards to get back to the house to put on the reception for the invited gentry.

Mary's heart felt heavy. Lady Elizabeth Glendenning had been a wonderful employer. She had taught her how to swim and had Mr Stevens teach her arithmetic, English and history and even taught her how to speak properly. For how the people in High Society conducted themselves she had had a ringside seat. The thought brought sadness mixed with the melancholy of the day as for the first time in her life she felt the sin of envy. Mary knew she had the skills to pass herself off as part of the upper echelons of society, it wasn't that difficult, but the chance would never come her way. The next best thing would be a lady's maid but now there was no need for a lady's maid at Hartford House.

She would find other employment. Lady Elizabeth even though she was on her death bed took the trouble to write her a letter of recommendation.

Chapter Six

Mary sat on her bed and slipped off her leather soled ankle boots without metal tips. The sad day had been long. So many to feed after the funeral when she would have preferred to be in her room alone with her thoughts.

A knock at the door brought her thoughts back to the present. She stood and with heavy steps made her way to the door and opened it to find Polly the kitchen maid.

"Master says he wants to see you in the study, Mary."

"Thank you." *Well, this is it. He'll either offer me the parlour maid job or send me away. He doesn't need to bother because I'm going anyway. I can get another job with the letter of recommendation.* Mary put her boots on. Butterflies in her tummy and a racing heartbeat went with her to Sir Edward's study on the ground floor with its view of the ornate gardens at the back of Hartford House. The sun was on the cusp of setting, colouring the sky shades of orange and giving a sepia hue to land. A nice evening after a horrible day.

"Ah, Dunsford, come in," said Sir Edward. "What are we to do with you?"

"I wish to give in my notice, sir."

"Really? I was about to offer you the parlour maid post and Mrs Jones isn't getting any younger. One day soon she will retire and I shall need a good housekeeper with my wife gone."

"Thank you, sir. I shall work whatever notice is required and then leave." Mary let out a sigh of relief that she had stood up for herself. Her relief felt tinged with caution. On the day of his wife's funeral, it didn't seem right for him to concern himself with a servant's position.

That would normally be left to Mr Stevens and Mrs Jones.

Sir Edward stepped over to the study door and turned a key in the lock.

Mary's heart thumped. She could see a horrible expression on his face as he turned towards her.

"Of course, but we have unfinished business before you leave, Dunsford." He stepped towards her.

Mary backed away but he was between her and the locked door. She could see no other way out. What he wanted was clear to her. Mary had never been with a man or boy before.

She hadn't even kissed one except once when she kissed Johnny Sandes on the cheek which seemed so long ago.

Sir Edward closed the gap and grabbed her holding her tight against him. "I can make your life very comfortable or very bad." He forced his lips against hers. She bit his lip, struggled and managed to step back from him. He lunged at her again. In a desperate swipe she clawed her fingernails down his cheek drawing blood. He put his hand to his face and bellowed.

Mary ran for the door, managed to unlock it, and get out into the corridor. As if she had wings on her feet she ran upstairs, into her room and dragged the washstand in front of the door.

Her mind raced as she tried to think what to do. If she went to Mrs Jones or Mr Stevens, they would do nothing because there was nothing they could do. They would lose their jobs if they intervened. Her ears tuned to any noise in the corridor outside but detected none. She expected him to come to her door, maybe break it down. But no sound came from outside.

As she sat on the bed a plan began to unfold. She would leave in the morning and take the letter of recommendation that Lady Elizabeth had given her. Though she wanted to keep the diamond earrings she would need to find accommodation and eat until she found a suitable position perhaps in Dorset or Wiltshire. If she could get to Southampton, she would board a train for Dorchester on the newly opened line. Only if her money ran out would she sell the earrings . On a salary of thirty pounds a year she had saved some and bought herself a few good clothes that she could wear away from the house.

Mary sat up all night listening to every creak and groan that the house made as it settled itself.

***

When the first rays of sun crept over the windowsill, Mary washed in her basin and packed her belongings in a leather bag that Lady Elizabeth had given her. She took her life savings of ten pounds eleven shillings and seven pence and the earrings from her hiding place under the floorboards and put it all at the bottom of the pocket in her black coat with the rabbit fur collar. She loved her distinctive coat and felt some comfort as she pulled it on.

Only Polly would be up at this hour, lighting the fires, she hoped.

The washstand scraped over the floorboards as she pushed it clear of the door. With her heart rate making blood sing in her ears, she peeked out into the corridor. Clear. On tiptoe she descended the backstairs and left the house by the back door into the stable yard where to her surprise she saw the stable hand Andy.

"Morning' Mary. Where be you goin' at this time of the day?"

"I'm leaving, Andy. I'm not needed now that Lady Elizabeth has passed so I have to go and find employment elsewhere."

"Where?"

"I don't know yet. I'm going to Southampton and maybe go west on a train."

"A train? Oh my. That would be an adventure."

"Indeed, it will, Andy. Goodbye."

"Well good luck to you lass. It's a big old world out there. Be careful."

"Thank you, Andy."

Mary set off on the road to Southampton. By carriage with her mistress, it would take an hour, on foot she expected it would take all morning.

Chapter Seven

Mary sat on a bench at the railway station glad to take the weight off her feet after the eight mile walk into Southampton. A huge white clock with Roman numerals hung over the platform showed a quarter past three, the Dorchester train according to the stationmaster was three twenty-five. A few other passengers waited on the other benches while some stood looking down the line for the arrival of the steam train.

She watched as a uniformed policeman and a man in a bowler hat came along the platform and to her surprise stopped in front of her.

"Miss Mary Dunsford?" said the man in the bowler hat.

Mary stood. Both men towered over her five feet four inches. "Yes, sir." The fear that Sir Edward had reported her for scratching his face ran through her but she managed to stand straight and wait for what they had to say. How did they pick her out? Then she remembered her coat. There were few like it.

"Mary Dunsford, I am Sergeant Phillips of the Southampton Borough Police and I am arresting you on suspicion of stealing a pair of diamond earrings from Hartford House," said the bowler hatted man.

Mary stared at him. "Steal? I haven't stolen anything. I have a pair of earrings that Lady Elizabeth Glendenning gave to me. Sir Edward is a witness that she gave them to me. So are Mrs Jones and Brenda at the house."

"Let me see them."

Mary reached into her pocket and pulled out the earrings wrapped in a piece of cloth with her money.

""Hmmm," said Phillips taking the earrings from her and handing back the money which consisted of one five-pound note, five one-pound notes and the change.

"It's Sir Edward says you stole them, lass. You'll have to come with us," said the uniformed policeman who had a kinder face than his companion. He picked up her bag.

With an officer each side of her she left the platform wondering what she should do. If Sir Edward said she stole the earrings Mrs Jones and Brenda would tell the truth, or would they?

 Another five minutes and she would have been gone. How did they know she would be at the railway station? Then she remembered she told Andy where she was going. She hoped he wouldn't have ratted on her, but if it were her or his job then his choice would be her, she supposed.

At the police station at the Southampton Bargate which she remembered seeing from her time in the Workhouse, Philips took Mary to a uniformed sergeant sitting behind a high desk. A woman with a weasel face and a black dress stood next to him.

"Arrested on suspicion of stealing a pair of diamond earrings, sergeant. I need her searched." He put the earrings on the desk.

The weasel faced woman took Mary by the elbow, led her into a windowless room and closed the door.

"Strip," said the weasel.

Mary stared at her. "No!"

To her surprise the weasel left the room leaving Mary standing alone. At least she had stood up for herself.

The door opened and a large woman came in with the weasel. "Strip," said the large woman.

"No!"

In a flurry of arms Mary found herself pinned to the floor and hands pulling at her clothes. "All right, all right. I'll do it."

The women let her stand. They watched as she undressed. The weasel woman took the money from Mary's coat pocket and counted it out. "Seven pounds ten shillings and nine pence," said weasel slipping something into her own pocket.

Mary paid ten pence for her third-class train ticket so she knew she still had ten pounds ten shillings and nine pence. The weasel had taken three-pound notes. "Hey," objected Mary.

"Be quiet," said the large woman.

The jailors searched through her clothing and then allowed her to dress. Weasel took her back out to the sergeant and put the seven pounds, ten shillings and nine pence on the desk. She wrote the figures on a form and pushed it to Mary to sign.

"They've stolen my money," said Mary. "I had ten pounds, ten shillings and nine pence."

The sergeant looked over the desk at her and then at weasel and the large woman. "Is that so?"

"It is sir," said Mary.

"I didn't see how much she had," said the large woman, quickly.

Weasel shuffled on her feet.

Phillips stepped forward. Mary saw him pick up the form and then check the money. "Miss Dunsford is telling the truth. She had one five-pound note and five one-pound notes plus change."

Mary saw weasel turn pale.

"Empty your pockets," said the sergeant to the weasel.

She backed away.

Phillips grabbed hold of her. "Empty your pockets."

She took three-pound notes from her pocket and put them on the desk.

"I'll deal with you later," said the sergeant.

The large woman took Mary to a cell, made her take off her shoes and locked her in. Mary looked around the eight feet by eight feet room with a high barred window that let in some light. A bucket stood in a corner and a bunk with a blanket lay against the wall. As she sat on the hard bunk tears fell down her cheeks.

Chapter Eight

Mary gripped the dock rail of the Great Hall in Winchester castle making her knuckles turn white while two judges in their finery and a magistrate in a dark frock coat sat high above the assembled court for her trial at the Quarter Sessions. On the wall behind her was the fabled Round Table of King Arthur where it had hung for six hundred years as witness to what was called justice. Though King Arthur was legend, not real, Mary wished one of his knights would ride into the court and rescue her. The Bloody Assizes of Judge Jeffries held in this sombre hall had seen many men sentenced to death for the Monmouth Rebellion. Mr Stevens had told her about it in one of her lessons. She never imagined that one day she would stand here. Mary's alleged crime was far less serious hence the Quarter Sessions rather than the twice-yearly Assizes though the outcome for her looked dire.

She didn't expect justice to be done. Mrs Jones and Brenda had denied being present when Lady Elizabeth gave Mary the earrings. Though it hurt her that they lied she understood why. Sir Edward held considerable power over them and everyone else at Hartford House.

"Mary Dunsford, do you plead guilty or not guilty to the theft of a pair of diamond earrings the property of Sir Edward Glendenning?" said the clerk of the court dressed in a black gown and white wig.

"Not guilty, sir," said Mary in as strong a voice as she could manage though her words were lost in the vast hall. She glanced over at the twelve men of the jury; a respectable group of local traders she understood them to be but they looked very solemn to her.

Mary sat down, next to a matron with a frosty face.

A black robed man in a wig stood and addressed the court. "Milord, gentlemen of the jury, this is a simple case of thievery by someone in a trusted position made more shameful by the fact that it was committed on the day of the funeral of the defendant's employer. Call Sir Edward Glendenning."

Sir Edward marched into the room, into the witness box and swore the oath with the Bible in his right hand.

"Sir Edward, do you recognise these earrings?" said the prosecutor holding up the diamond earrings.

An usher took them to Sir Edward.

"I do. I bought them for my wife on her thirtieth birthday."

"And did you, sir, give these diamond earrings to the defendant?"

"Of course not. Why would I?"

"Did your wife give the earrings to the defendant?"

"No. How ridiculous to suggest that such a valuable pair of earrings would be given to a maid."

"When did you last see the earrings?"

"On the day of the funeral. They were in my wife's jewellery box. I was overtaken with grief and looked in her box to try to gain some comfort from them and to remember the times she wore them." He choked back a sob.

Mary stared at him. Three months had passed since she was arrested and Sir Edward's facial wounds that she inflicted had healed. She could see he was giving a fine act.

"And when did you find the earrings missing?"

"The next day. I went to the jewellery box to put it in a safe place and found the diamond earrings were not there. I noticed that they were missing because they were my wife's favourite earrings and I wanted to have a last look at them before I put them away."

"And then what happened?"

"I called for Dunsford and discovered that she had left the house that morning, early, with her belongings. One of my staff told me he had seen her and she stated she was going to Southampton to catch a train to Dorchester. She didn't give notice. She just left. I informed the police."

Mary had no money; she was unrepresented so she had to defend herself.

"Sir Edward, you were present when Lady Elizabeth gave me the earrings. So were Mrs Jones and Brenda."

"Not only are you a thief, but you are also a liar," said Sir Edward.

Mary pondered whether she should raise the night he tried to force himself on her as that was the reason she left in a hurry the next morning. She was sure he would deny it and if the allegation alienated the jury against her then that would make her position even worse and decided against it. There was nothing she could say about her arrest.

If she insisted on calling Brenda and Mrs Jones, they would either lie to the court and risk a long jail sentence for perjury if discovered or if they told the truth they would be unemployed and probably not believed by the jury. Their positions were as dire as her own so she decided she would not call them.

The judge summed up which took less than five minutes before the jury left the court. The matron took Mary to the cells to await the verdict and she had just sat down on a bunk when she was called back to the court.

The jury foreman read out the verdict. "Guilty."

Mary's stomach turned oily. She knew the punishment for a maid stealing from her employer would be harsh to send a signal to other maids.

The judge intoned over his beaky nose. "Mary Dunsford, you have been found guilty of stealing a pair of diamond earrings from your deceased employer on the day of her funeral. Such a wicked act must be punished severely. You are sentenced to seven years transportation to Australia. Next."

Mary's heart sank. Her feet descended the stairs to the cells as if they were made of lead.

Chapter Nine

Mary sat on a bench in the back of a closed in cart alongside five other prisoners on her side and six on the other side. Manacles around her ankles and handcuffs on her wrists cut into her skin. A weasel like face on the opposite bench stared at her. Mary could feel the venom coming her way. The woman was in chains too.

"It's a long way to Australia and there's always the risk of an accident," hissed the weasel. In the cells Mary had heard that the jailer was sentenced to seven years transportation for stealing her money in the police station. It appeared a person in the employ of the Crown stealing from prisoners in a police station also carried a severe penalty.

The cart bumped over the rough road to Portsmouth. Only a little fresh air drifted in from a small grill above the back door. The smell of twelve bodies that had been in jail for several months now cramped into a poorly ventilated space hung in the air. A boy on the opposite bench, Mary thought he must be around eleven years old, coughed continually. Jail fever was what she'd heard it called.

After a long journey that to Mary seemed to have lasted all day the cart stopped and the door opened. Mary gulped in the fresh air and noticed a tang of salt in it. The prisoners shuffled out of the cart and lined up on the quayside. A sorry row of human jetsam about to be cast to the far side of the world.

A longboat moored to the key rose and fell in the swell. Four sailors with oars sat on board staring at the prisoners. Mary detected pity in their eyes. A constable chivvied the prisoners to the boat where they boarded with difficulty due to their chains.

Mary gazed out into the harbour to see many masted ships lying at anchor. One of them would take her to Australia and a fate she did not want to think about. In the jail many stories were told about what happened to prisoners in Australia and for pretty young women it seemed they fared the worse.

The longboat tied up alongside a huge ship. A door halfway down the hull had steps leading up from the water. To Mary the climb appeared dangerous as the steps rose and fell in the swell. The sailors helped the prisoners off the longboat onto a small landing at the bottom of the steps. Mary found herself standing next to the weasel with the woman nearest to the hull and Mary next to the water.

Suddenly the weasel barged her shoulder against Mary knocking her off balance and off the landing into the water. The chains took Mary under before she had chance to grab anything to save herself.

Down and down, she sank into the murky depths of Portsmouth harbour. She held her breath while she struggled but the descent continued. Her lungs groaned as if they were on fire. The need to suck in a deep breath became almost overwhelming but she knew when that happened it would be the end of her. She carried on struggling in a desperate attempt to save her life. The chains on her ankles slipped off as she wrenched and tugged at them, lubricated by the seawater. With her feet free she kicked for the surface holding her handcuffed hands out in front. This was not the style that Lady Elizabeth had taught her but it worked. High above she could see the daylight filtering through and the dark shape of the ship's keel.

Mary broke surface on the opposite side of the ship from which she had fallen. She gripped a rib on the hull to hold herself up and looked around for help. Her mouth opened and was about to shout for help when she stopped and closed it again. If she called out, she would be rescued and taken to Australia for whatever nightmare awaited her. If she kept quiet and managed not to drown or freeze to death, she may manage to make it to the shore and go into hiding. Everyone would expect she perished in the depths and she knew they may not be wrong. Death, Australia, or the chance to live were the options her frenzied mind turned over and over. Mary decided on death or freedom.

About fifty yards from the stern of the prison ship she could see a fishing boat anchored that appeared to be unoccupied. A glance up the side of the ship gave her hope, nobody looked down. To steady herself she sucked in deep breaths. With effort she managed to slip out of her dress by tearing the stitching at the shoulders, bundled it, and held in her handcuffed hands.

And then with hope and fear in equal measures she ducked under and swam for the fishing boat. With the need to keep her head below the water finding the fishing boat would be difficult and she could come up in an open space and be spotted. Her dress held out in front created drag but she held on to it. Wandering around in her underwear if she made it to the shore would not be an option. She would struggle on for if she were captured it would all be for nothing and Australia would beckon after a flogging.

Mary kicked like a frog as hard as she could and kept her arms out straight. How far she had come she didn't know but she had to come up for air. Hoping that she was far enough from the prison ship not to be spotted she trod water, raised her head, and found herself only about ten yards from the fishing boat. She had to put the boat between her and the ship to avoid being seen boarding so she dived again and swam to the far side of the fishing boat. Clinging to the side she listened for any sign of life aboard and heard none. With a heave she threw her dress over the gunwale. He body felt like a ton weight after her time in the water and the struggle to get herself aboard took all her strength but she made a supreme effort and managed. Once on the deck she ducked low so she couldn't be seen from the ship.

The fishing boat cabin's door stood ajar swinging in the swell. Mary crawled towards it, leaving her dress on the deck she wore only a pair of drawers, a threadbare chemise, and no shoes. Her boots were stolen in prison and all she had worn on her feet were a pair of canvas sandals that had come off in the water.

In the dark cabin she saw a blanket on a bunk covering something. The cold water, fear, and relief at having survived made her shiver uncontrollably. She grabbed the blanket, threw it around her shoulders and then stifled a scream.

An old man lay on the bunk. He opened his eyes; she could see he was as surprised to see her as she him.

"What the. . ." said the man as he sat up suddenly and banged his head on the cabin roof.

"Sorry, I. . . Sorry," was all she managed to say. Her hands cuffed in front of her were on plain view and she had no way of hiding them. She could see the old man staring at them.

Mary cast her eyes down and for the first time since getting out of the water saw her ankles. They bled. Forcing off the manacles had stripped the skin.

The man swung his feet off the bunk and sat upright rubbing his head. He looked her up and down. "I reckon you be off that prison ship headed for Van Diemen's land."

"What if I am?" said Mary summoning up as much defiance as a cold and wet young woman in her drawers and chemise could.

"Then what I have to say Missy is. . . well done lass. You looks like you've had a hard time of it. Up for'ard through that hatch you'll find a pair of britches and a woolly. You'd best be putting them on afore you dies of the cold."

Mary pulled open a door in the bow and stepped into a small cabin that held some line, lamps, fishing paraphernalia and a shelf on which she found some clothing. She slipped out of her wet underwear and put on a pair of pants that were too big for her but had a leather belt that she tightened around her narrow waist. A thick grey woollen jumper soon had her feeling warmer. She stepped back into the main cabin to find the old man boiling a kettle on an iron stove.

"Looks like you could do with a hot drink lass. And I've some bread and cheese. No fish, ain't been out today. Going out tonight." He opened a cupboard and lifted down a loaf and a piece of cheese which he cut with a knife from his belt. He placed the bread and cheese on a small table and poured the kettle into a teapot. "Get this down you."

Mary ate the bread and cheese stuffing it into her so fast she got the hiccups. The old man poured ale from a bottle into a tin mug and handed it to her. Two handed because of the cuffs, she quaffed it in one swallow to wash down the obstruction. Feeling better after the bread, cheese, and ale she wondered what was to happen next. The man didn't look as if he would turn her in though there was usually a reward for capturing an escaped felon. He poured out a tin mug of tea. There was no sugar or milk but it still tasted good to Mary.

"So, lass, what's your story?"

"I was to be transported for stealing a pair of earrings. But I didn't steal them. The Master accused me because I wouldn't. . . er. . . you know."

"Yes lass, I knows. So how did you get away?"

"One of the prisoners who had a grudge against me pushed me into the water as we were boarding the ship. I sank but managed to get the leg irons off and swim here. They must think I drowned."

"You is a plucky young 'un if you managed to do that. I'm fishing tonight but I can put you ashore in the morning. After that, you're on your own girl. I can't help you any further. I ain't got no place other than this here boat."

"I don't know how to thank you enough sir."

"You don't need to thank me and you'll be safe with me. I'm well past bothering a pretty young woman. Now let's get those bracelets off you and clean up your ankles. Bastards manacling a lass."

The old man went forward into the bow cabin and came back with a hammer, an iron rod, and a short thick length of chain. He placed the chain in a heap on the cabin floor. "Now put your hands on the chain."

Mary looked at the hammer and iron rod wondering how the man would break the rigid metal cuffs that were held together with a bar. With little choice other than to trust him, she put her hands on the chain so that the bar that connected the two cuffs was exposed.

The old man put the rod on the bar and whacked it with the hammer. A shock of pain ran up Mary's arms and she let out a scream.

"Shush," said the man. The connecting bar didn't budge. "This won't work. Somewhere I have a file." He went back into the forward cabin. Mary could hear banging and rattling as he moved stuff around. He came back with a metal file.

"Will that get through?" said Mary, dubious about whether it could cut through the bar.

"If it don't then you'll have to stay handcuffed."

Mary put her hands on the chain again. The man knelt and began filing the bar. He stopped every few minutes to gather his breath and then continued. She could see it was having an effect but how long it would take worried her because the old man was tiring. He persevered and eventually the file broke through. Mary found her hands no longer held together with the bar though each still held the cuffs.

"I can't get the bracelets off but at least you can use your hands now."

"Thank you, said Mary."

"Tomorrow, when I put you ashore, I'll take you to a blacksmith I trust and he'll get the cuffs off you."

"I don't know how to thank you enough. I don't even know your name."

"The name's Harry, I don't need to know yours. Tonight, you can help me fish."

***

Mary sat in the cockpit of the fishing boat under a sky filled with stars and a half-moon. Over the side she dangled a handline Harry had baited with feathers for mackerel. In the moonlight she could see the outline of the Isle of Wight. The boat bobbed on the swell with the sail furled and the boom tied down. Around her shoulders she wore the blanket over the thick woolly but still the cold seeped in.

Harry sat with a line over the other side of the boat.

Suddenly, Mary felt her line twitch. She pulled it in and to her surprise six mackerel were on the hooks.

"Unhook and over again," said Harry drawing in his line that also had several mackerel.

They put the mackerel into a barrel and carried on fishing. In the next hour Mary brought in twenty-seven mackerel.

She didn't see how many Harry had but it was at least twice as many.

Without any more bites Harry pulled in his line and beckoned Mary to do the same. He hoisted the sail and steered the boat further inland towards the island and then anchored about two hundred yards offshore. He set up a fishing rod with a single hook and baited it before handing it to Mary to fish off the port side. He then set up another rod and cast it out away from the boat.

A huge tug at the line made Mary squeal with delight and surprise. Harry squatted alongside her. Following his gentle instructions, she managed to get the big fish to the side of the boat where he used a gaff to bring it aboard.

"Reckon he's around seven pounds. Sea bass. Well done lass."

Mary caught three more bass before the sun climbed above the horizon sending a glow across the flat water.

Harry sailed the boat back around the Island to the mainland and beached her on a shingle beach in a cove. Mary recognised it. This was the beach where she used to come with Lady Elizabeth to swim.

A bearded man with a horse and cart jumped off his cart and came down the beach to the boat.

"Good catch, Harry?" said the man.

"Mackerel and some sea bass."

Mary jumped down from the boat.

"Looks like you caught a mermaid too, Harry!" guffawed the bearded man.

"Help me load the fish and then I have a job for you," said Harry taking the man by the elbow and leading him to the boat.

The two men carried the heavy barrel of fish up to the cart.

Harry waved to Mary to come up to the cart.

She trod carefully through the shingle. "What's happening?"

"Get your dress and come with us," said Harry.

Mary made her way back to the boat, grabbed her now dry and ripped dress and came back up the shingle. "Where are we going?"

"To see the blacksmith to get those cuffs off you," said Harry.

Mary looked at the bearded man. He seemed to have taken it all in his stride. But would he turn her in for a reward? She had to trust that Harry knew the answer to that question.

The horse and cart trundled through the village to a barn on the outskirts. She kept low in the back of the cart next to the fish and held her nose. The bearded man pulled up the rig at the barn and climbed down. Mary peered over the edge of the cart and saw a big man with a leather apron in front of a forge hammering a piece of glowing metal.

"Come on down," said Harry getting off the cart.

She climbed down looking all around.

"Thanks Phil," said Harry to the bearded man. "See you same place tomorrow morning and you can pay me then."

The bearded man nodded, tapped his horse on its flank and drove away leaving Harry and Mary with the blacksmith.

"Can you get these cuffs off this young lady, Joseph?"

The blacksmith stepped forward and took Mary's hands in his huge ones. She could feel they were as hard as the leather apron he wore.

"I reckon," said the blacksmith. "Don't tell me nothin'. Less I know less I can be asked." Still holding her hands, he led her into the barn and stopped at an anvil. The barn smelled of coal from a huge pile at the far end. He rummaged around in a pile of tools and came back with a hammer and a spike. Holding her left hand, he placed it on the anvil so the lock was on the hard surface. Then he whacked it with the spike. The lock snapped and fell of her hand though the shock vibrated up her arm.

He repeated the process with the other cuff and it came off with the first blow too.

"All right young lady, that's all I can do for you," said Harry. "I'll leave you here. You can keep the clothes."

"Thank you, Harry."

Harry wandered off back in the direction from where they had come.

"So, what's your plan?" asked the blacksmith. Mary noticed he had a soft voice for such a big man.

"Don't know."

"Well, you can't go around looking like a scarecrow. Come with me. The missus may be able to help you with some clothes and I think you'll need a pair of shoes."

Mary couldn't help feeling that there were so many good people in the world willing to help her. She followed the blacksmith into a house behind the barn. Wisteria grew around the door and roses bloomed in the garden from where she could see the sea.

The blacksmith pushed open the door, Mary followed him into a small hallway. "Gwen we've got a visitor."

A woman opened an internal door. Mary could see it was a kitchen. She wore a pinny, grey dress and a mob cap. Using the pinny, she wiped flour from her hands.

"And who be she?" said the woman Gwen.

"A stray that Harry found."

"Another one! Humph. Well, she looks like one. Come here girl."

Mary approached Gwen wondering if she would be the one to turn her in.

"What an unholy mess you are in, girl. Joseph, go back to work, I'll take it from here."

Joseph went outside. Mary went into the kitchen with Gwen.

"When did you last eat?"

"Last night, Ma'am. Harry gave me some bread and cheese."

"Well, that won't keep you going for long."

Gwen filled a pan with oats and water and put it on the range which gave off a lot of heat that Mary was glad for after the night on the sea.

"I doubt Joseph asked you any questions. He doesn't ask them and he should. Now tell me dear, what sort of pickle have you got yourself in? I can see from your wrists and ankles that you've been manacled."

Mary found herself having to trust someone she didn't know, again. "I was sentenced to transportation for seven years for stealing a pair of earrings from my employer but I didn't steal them. She gave them to me."

"Then why did she say you stole them?"

"She didn't. She died. Her husband accused me because I wouldn't let him. . ."

"Hmmm one of those. And you escaped? Not many manage that. Not even big strong men never mind a slip of a girl like you. How did you get away?"

"I was pushed into the water by another prisoner and managed to swim to Harry's fishing boat. I hope the authorities think I drowned."

"So do I," said Gwen stirring the oats. "Would you be the maid from Hartford House?"

"Er. . . yes."

"Hmmm. That's not far from here. You'd best get as far away from this area as you can in case you are recognised. I heard about what happened. I know the housekeeper, Mrs Jones."

"Nobody spoke up for me from the house. They were too afraid of Sir Edward."

"That's what I heard. I knew Lady Elizabeth too. Well not personally of course but I knew of her. So sad. And so sad to have been married to that devil Edward Glendenning."

"I don't know what I 'm going to do now."

"We'll get you scrubbed up and fed before we decide what to do with you."

Gwen poured the oats into a bowl and put it on the table in front of Mary. She ate it without speaking. As her tummy filled with the warm oats her hopes of survival and freedom rose.

Chapter Ten

Mary stood in front of the dressing table mirror. She ran
her hand through her neatly cut and clean hair, the cleanest
it had been since the day she was arrested. The dress that
Gwen gave her fitted after the woman made a few
alterations to take it in. The older woman's waist being
considerably wider than Mary's but their heights were
similar.

Gwen fussed around making a few more adjustments to
the dress. Though a plain grey, Mary could tell it was a
quality garment. "It's so good of you to let me have this
dress. You don't even know me and yet you are so kind."

"The world is a cruel place for those without means. I
would hope that if I were in need, someone would help
me. It's the Christian thing to do."

Mary couldn't hold herself back, threw her arms
around Gwen and burst into tears.

"Now, now girl. It'll be all right. We'll get you to
somewhere safe. Don't worry."

***

As she lay in the clean bed listening to an owl somewhere
calling its mate or perhaps just giving its mournful cry, she

thought of Harry out on the water fishing, the man with the cart who had brought her here to the blacksmith and Gwen. And the vision of what the hell would be aboard the ship now heading for Australia kept drifting into her mind. The weasel had tried to steal her money and tried to drown her but the weasel had unintentionally saved her by her actions. Much to Mary's surprise she felt a tinge of pity for the weasel.

Her dreams took her back to Highfields House and Johnny Sandes. In this dream they were both grown and Johnny courted her with a bunch of flowers from the walled garden. When she woke with the sun creeping over the windowsill she wondered how Johnny had fared. Had he married? He would be a catch for any well-connected young lady. She wasn't sure if it was the dire straits she found herself in that she clung to the thoughts of Johnny. They were just children when last they saw each other but she had a strong urge to see him again. How she would manage that without being caught she had no idea.

Mary made her way down the rickety steps of the cottage to the kitchen where she found Gwen baking bread.

"Sit down lass and I'll make you some bacon and eggs. Then we're going for a trip to the New Forest. I have a sister there who is the housekeeper at a fine estate and we'll see if we can get you employed there as a maid. I doubt it will be a lady's maid post, you may have to settle for scullery but you need work and you need to be away from this area because Sir Edward or one of his staff may see you."

"I'll do any honest job, Ma'am."

"I ain't a Ma'am lass. I'm Gwen."

***

Mary, with a tarpaulin over her, sat in the back of the blacksmith's wagon pulled by a shire horse called Gertie. Gwen sat up front with the reins in one hand and a whip in the other which she used to coax the horse in the right directions.

Though cramped the journey was far less fearful than the one from the prison to the ship and Mary felt safe in her hideaway and trust in the woman up front.

How far was Lyndhurst in the New Forest from where they were was a mystery to Mary but Gwen told her it would take around eight hours in the cart. With no guarantee of a job when they arrived it did not distract from the hope that she would gain employment even if it was a lowly scullery maid post. The cart swayed and bumped over the roads through the countryside and then Mary was aware of the bustle outside.

"We're going through Southampton now," said Gwen. "Keep down in case anyone recognises you."

Mary had no intention of raising her head above the tarpaulin.

The bustle of the town gave way to the quiet clip clop of Gertie and the silence of the countryside again with an occasional sound of horses hooves as riders and carts passed in the opposite direction.

At last, the cart stopped. "You can come out now," said Gwen pulling the tarpaulin off Mary.

Mary tried to stand but her legs were seized up. It took a struggle to stand and her thigh muscles groaned in complaint as did her back and shoulders. Gwen helped her down. Mary stretched her arms and legs and walked around the cart only then seeing where they were.

The cart and horse were outside a small cottage with a garden at the front surrounded by a brown painted picquet fence. Roses surrounded the door. A chimney smoked in the centre of a thatched roof. Mary thought how beautiful it looked.

Over the fields a huge house caught the last rays of the day making it look orange as it stood in landscaped gardens. It would take several groundsmen to keep the estate in such a beautiful condition. An idea slipped into her mind. *Why did they have to be grounds 'men'?*

Gwen took Mary by the arm and led her to the cottage door where she knocked on the brass hand shaped knocker.

A woman similar in appearance to Gwen opened the door. "Oh my! Gwen. I wasn't expecting you."

"Hello Angharad. I'd like you to meet my friend Mary. She needs a job and I was wondering if you could assist her."

"Come in." Angharad stepped aside and waved in her visitors to a parlour with a fire in the hearth, stone flagged floor, mullioned window with a view of a back garden, a rocking chair and a sofa."

From outside at the back Mary heard someone sawing.

Angharad gestured for Mary and Gwen to sit on the sofa while she took the rocking chair. "Well, I think you need to tell me what all this about."

Mary tried to pull the sleeves of her dress down to cover the marks on her wrists but she could see that Angharad had already noticed them.

"Mary is in a little trouble."

"Little?" said Angharad. "Those marks are the marks of manacles. Come on, out with it!"

Mary decided to throw herself on the mercy of this woman she had never met. If she was the sister of Gwen then she could be trusted though she had no choice to do anything else. "I escaped from a transportation ship headed for Australia. I was falsely accused of stealing a pair of diamond earrings from my employer but I am innocent."

"Hmmm," said Angharad stroking her chin. Mary noticed how blue were her eyes and they seemed to be boring into her.

"She needs a job, Angharad. Her employer was Sir Edward Glendenning, well his wife, Mary was her lady's maid. She gave Mary the earrings. Sir Edward wanted more from Mary than Mary was prepared to give if you understand what I mean."

"Sadly, I understand all too well. Thank God we don't have that problem here."

Angharad stood and stepped over to a bureau where she dropped the lid and reached inside. She came out with a small Bible. "Mary, I want you to swear on this Bible that you are innocent. If you lie you know you shall be damned for eternity."

Sunday mornings at the Workhouse always included a church service that the inmates were compelled to attend. In her time she had seen three vicars at the church and each one preached fire and brimstone. Most of the time she didn't believe God would punish people the way the priests claimed but sometimes in the dark of night those stories came to frighten her.

Mary put her hand on the Bible. She looked Angharad in the eyes. "I swear on the Holy

Bible that I am innocent of stealing the earrings or anything else."

"Good," said Angharad. "Then I will take that as true. We have no vacancy for a lady's maid and such posts tend to be chosen by the Lady herself rather than the housekeeper or butler. I am authorised to hire lower ranked maids and we do have a kitchen maid post to fill at fifteen pounds per year."

Mary was grateful for any post. Not wanting to push her luck but also not wanting to miss the opportunity she decided to ask. "Ma'am, I have some knowledge of gardening. If there was a post in the gardens that I could fill I would do an excellent job."

Angharad shook her head. "Mr Williams hires the groundsmen. It's not unknown for females to work in the gardens but it isn't common. I don't know if there are vacancies."

Gwen put her hand over her mouth. Mary thought she was trying to stifle a laugh. It wasn't that funny to want a job in the gardens, she thought.

"I really would do an excellent job, Ma'am."

Angharad smiled. "Well, I'll have to ask Mr Williams."

This time Gwen failed to stop herself from laughing.

Mary felt hurt. She liked Gwen but mocking her was not nice, in her opinion.

Angharad stood and walked over to a door which she pulled open to reveal a small lobby with a door leading off. "Fred, Gwen is here with a friend I'd like you to meet."

A man in his forties with a grey beard and a saw in his hand appeared.

"This is my husband, Fred Williams and this is Mary. . . er don't know her last name."

"Hello Gwen, hello Mary," said Fred with a gentle voice. He put the saw on the side of the hearth. "Just cutting some trellis work. Haven't seen you for ages Gwen. How's Joseph, still swinging that hammer?"

"He's fine, Fred."

"Fred," said Angharad. "Mary has a small problem. She's on the run from the authorities who want to transport her to Australia for a crime she didn't commit. So, as Head Groundsman, can you employ her as a groundsman, er grounds woman?"

Mary gulped. Angharad was direct and no wonder it was funny when they were discussing the gardening job with her husband being the head gardener.

"You done any gardening before?" asked Fred.

"Yes, sir. I worked in gardens when I was at the Workhouse and I helped Lady Elizabeth in her garden."

"It's hard work in all weathers. It won't be like helping your Mistress. This will involve digging, grass cutting, carrying wood and just about every back-breaking job you could think of. Wouldn't you be better off working in the house?"

"If you will give a chance to show you that I can do all that, I would be grateful, sir."

Fred nodded. "All right. You're hired. If you are on the run from the police and prison authorities what are we going to put your name down as because it can't be the real one."

"I'm Mary Dunsford but I don't know what to take as another last name."

Angharad joined in the discussion. "Best keep the name Mary or you'll get confused if someone calls you another name and you don't respond quick enough. For your last name I suggest Smith. You can't go wrong with that."

"All right. Mary Smith, you are employed as third groundsman, woman, on fifteen pounds per year on the Dolby Estate."

"Thank you, sir."

Chapter Eleven

Hampshire, England April 1850

Mary sat on a barrel in the orangery of Dolby House thinning the Spring cuttings thinking of the time that passed since she jumped ship and found sanctuary on this estate in the New Forest. Fred Williams and his wife Angharad had helped her though there was nothing in it for them except danger if it emerged who Mary was and they had helped her hide from the authorities.

She liked the garden work even in the winter and the wet days. She'd grown strong. Though her hands were rough from the toil she had blossomed into an attractive young lady who would turn the head of any young man. Because of her past, she knew her chances of meeting and marrying a good man were few. An occasional daydream drifted into her mind about Johnny but she knew he was the past and not the future. She had no shortage of admirers but they were not decent men and their intentions were not honourable. For now, she was happy to put the idea of romance aside and concentrate on her work.

Working on the land meant she seldom encountered the landowner, Lord Chegwidden but his wife Lady Eleanor was a frequent visitor to the greenhouses and orangery. Mary had found sanctuary and had worked her way up to a position in the grounds staff to have charge of a small team responsible for the flower beds, greenhouses, and orangery. She had her own accommodation over the stable block that had a parlour cum kitchen and a bedroom.

The orangery door opening made Mary turn to see who had come in and saw Lady Eleanor with a worried look on her face. She lifted the tray of seedlings from her knee, stood and curtsied.

"Mary, Mr Williams suggested I speak to you."

Mary's heart sank. What had she done or what had Lady Eleanor discovered? The woman usually had a bright smile but today she looked as if there was a problem and that problem could be Mary.

"Yes, Milady?"

"We are having a June ball. It's the last Saturday in June so we have over two months."

Mary's shoulders sagged with relief. A ball was a major event so no wonder Milady was worried though what that had to do with Mary she didn't know.

"Mary, I will need lots and lots of flowers for the displays and I would like a bed of colourful ones along the drive. Mr Williams said it would be best for you to work with me on this rather than go through him. He will be busy with the other aspects of the grounds to get them ready."

"Yes Milady."

"I shall rely on your advice as to what we should plant along the drive. For the displays I want huge multi-coloured flowers and I shall leave it to you to decide on what they should be. It is so good to have a woman gardener; women have an affinity with design much better than men. And I've been impressed with your work."

"Thank you, Milady." Mary felt a burst of pride run through her. She was to be trusted to make decisions that would reflect on the estate and her. Mr Williams had put that work her way when he could easily have taken all the credit himself.

***

By the middle of June the driveway to Dolby House was a riot of colour. Down each side between the lime trees were beds of geraniums, iris, lupins, cornflowers, love-in-a-mist, and peonies. Her brief was to lay beds of bright colours and she had certainly achieved it although she knew that a purist gardener may look with contempt on the extraordinary collection she had planted. Lady Eleanor liked it and that was all that mattered to Mary.

In the orangery and greenhouses, she had grown lilies and other semi-tropical plants that she had obtained from Kew Gardens on a visit there with Lady Eleanor. Mary had come to understand that social position can unlock many doors included those of the Royal Botanic Gardens. These plants together with roses from the rose gardens would provide sweet scented displays in the house.

***

The estate was a bustle of activity on the morning of the ball. Mary and her team cut the flowers for the displays and ensured the ones on the drive were dead headed and in prime condition.

Dolby House had a massive ballroom with two huge chandeliers and a stage built at one end to accommodate the orchestra. The flower displays hung from metal baskets on the walls. A few tables around the perimeter of the room held vases with more flowers. The sprung wooden floor had a polished sheen that the maids had buffed without beeswax. Lady Eleanor did not want the odour of beeswax to compete with the scent of the flowers.

Mary managed a peek from her room over the stables as the carriages began to arrive at eight thirty. The sun hung low in the sky on this last Saturday in June just over a week after the longest day. The late evening light gave the driveway flowers an extra burst of colour making Mary beam with pride. That afternoon Lady Eleanor had made the effort to find her and congratulate her for the driveway and the display inside.

It had been a long day, indeed a long week for Mary preparing the flowers but her work was not yet done. For the ball she was pressed into service to help. In between looking at the grand carriages she dressed in a long black dress, white pinny and white lace cap. To cover her work worn hands she wore white gloves. Her role was to carry champagne on trays around the ballroom and later in the evening, help with the food. Charlie, the youngest footman had a broken foot due to getting it run over by a cart leaving Jeremiah the senior footman on his own so he needed her help. Nobody noticed a maid, or so she hoped. Though she had blossomed since escaping the ship anyone who knew her well would still recognise her and if that person reported her to the police she would be on the way to Australia.

She hurried across the stable yard and into the house where she found Mr Templeton, the butler and Angharad the housekeeper filling champagne glasses. Jeremiah took a tray and headed out into the corridor.

"Ah there you are Mary. Please take a tray into the ballroom and then come back for more when you've given those out," said Angharad. "Oh, and Megs has had some bad news. Her mother in Manchester is poorly and I've given her permission to go to her in the morning. I'd like you to step in as parlour maid until she comes back. It will probably be a few days."

"Yes, Mrs Williams." When others were around, she had to call Angharad Mrs Williams but when there were just the two of them it was always Angharad.

Mary carried a tray out into the corridor, across the white tiled entrance hall with its wooden chandelier and carved wooden staircase and into the ballroom. The crystal chandeliers were already lit although there was still light coming in from the rows of full-length windows down both sides of the room. The guests in their finery made a magnificent sight, thought Mary. Envy and jealousy were not in her nature but she felt a pang of regret that she had not been high born with the opportunity to participate in such a grand ball as a guest. If she had the clothes and the opportunity, she was sure she could pass herself off as one of the gentry after her education at Hartford House.

The ladies wore long dresses that Mary imagined cost a small fortune. Their necks and ears dripped with diamonds. Some of the men wore dark dress suits while others were in splendid army and navy uniforms.

She weaved through the guests with her tray and then stopped suddenly almost dropping the tray. A young man with ginger hair in Hussar's uniform of red pants and black jacket with gold braid stood talking with a group of older men. She had not seen Johnny

Sandes for many years but there was no mistaking that cheeky smile under the carrot top.

Keeping her hands on the tray steady against their attempts to shake, she offered the tray to the group of men and Johnny. The others took their glasses and continued to talk without bothering to look at the maid or say thank you. Johnny made the effort.

"Thank you," he said taking a champagne glass and smiling at Mary. His eyes lingered on her for a moment and then looked away.

Mary wasn't sure if she was happy or sad that he didn't recognise her. It would greatly complicate matters if he had. She was a wanted felon and it had been a long time since her friendship with Johnny. Now he wore an officer's uniform in the army of Queen Victoria and being in the service of the Crown he may have felt it necessary to turn her in if he knew that she had been sentenced to deportation. Why should he? They had lost contact and someone in his position was unlikely to follow the trials of the lower orders. Her crime hadn't been such that it would capture public interest. A maid stealing a pair of earrings was a minor crime; it wasn't minor for the alleged thief being transported to Australia for seven years hard labour and God knows what other nightmares.

With an empty tray she headed back to the kitchen and found Angharad alone.

"I'm sorry, I don't think I should go back into the ballroom. There's someone there who knows me. I don't think he recognised me but I can't be sure and if he sees me again, he may do so."

"Hmmm. Who is it? Does he have any grudges against you?"

"It's Johnny Sandes. I used to work in his parents' gardens and we were friends when we were children. No, he doesn't hold anything against me. But he's an officer in the army now and he may have to report me if he does recognise me. So, I'm sorry Angharad. Can I not go back out there, please?"

"Of course you can't go out there. The dancing is about to start so they won't be wanting much more champagne. Stay in the kitchen, you were down to help with the food after serving the champagne. Cook and her team will be back shortly. I told them to go outside and get some fresh air before the rush starts after the dancing stops."

Cook, Megs the parlour maid and three kitchen maids came in and set about laying out items for a buffet on trays.

"Sorry to hear about your Mum, Megs," said Mary.

"Thanks. She works in the cotton mill and all that dust plays havoc with her lungs. The message said she was extremely ill and may not last."

Mary put her hand on Megs shoulder. "Let's hope for the best."

"Mary, take this through to the dining room, please," said Cook pointing to a long silver tray on which a whole skinned salmon lay with lemon wedges and cucumber decorated around it.

Mary carried the salmon through to the dining room and placed it on the long centre table among other plates that held meat, chicken, and salads. She looked around the room decorated with her flowers and smiled. Soon the guests would come in and devour the sumptuous buffet. If she had been higher born it would be in a room like this that she would entertain guests. A portrait of a pretty lady in a Georgian dress looked down from over the marble fireplace. When installing the flowers, Lady Eleanor had told her the woman was Lord Chegwidden's great grandmother. Lady Eleanor had married well.

Outside the sun had set. Through the dining room window Mary could see the gardens illuminated with flambeaux. Mr Williams had done a grand job of arranging them exactly right so they showed off the perfectly manicured shrubs and lawns. A few guests milled around enjoying the cool evening air as the ballroom had become too stuffy with so many bodies and the candles in the chandeliers. The scent of flowers in the ballroom soon disappeared as the evening commenced.

As she made her way to the dining room door, she heard footsteps outside on the tiled floor. They weren't the steps of a maid or Angharad. These were the steps of a man's boots briskly walking.

Johnny Sandes came through the door. "I say, found the food. I'm sorry if I am being forward but I haven't eaten since this morning and frankly, I'm famished. Would it be impolite if I were to help myself to something just to keep me going until the buffet is served?"

Mary lowered her eyes to the floor and curtsied. "I'm sure Milady would have no objections, sir."

"Thank you." Johnny strode past and reached for a chicken leg. And then he suddenly turned.

Mary could see that he was staring at her. It made her blush and uncomfortable inside. Part of her wanted to run away into the kitchen as fast as she could but another part of her wanted to stay and hope that he would recognise her. What would she do if he did? He looked so handsome in his uniform it made her heart skip along at such a rate she wondered if he could hear it. Johnny would never mean her harm, would he?

He took a bite of the chicken leg and continued to look at her. "I'm sorry, please don't think I'm being rude but don't I know you?"

Mary longed to say yes, but enough common sense lingered for her to say, "I don't think so, sir."

"Hmmm." He took another bite of his chicken and turned his attention to a sausage.

Chapter Twelve

Mary dead headed the flowers in the orangery. Two weeks had passed since the ball.

She'd been doing two jobs since Megs left to see her mother. Angharad said she would be back that morning so Mary could concentrate on the garden.

It still troubled Mary whether she did the right thing telling Johnny that he was mistaken in thinking he knew her. A gnawing feeling in her tummy kept returning when she thought of how handsome he looked. After the meeting in the dining room, she had managed to avoid him for the rest of the evening and the last time she saw him it was from her room over the stables. He was boarding a carriage with two other soldiers.

Megs the scullery maid came into the orangery with an envelope addressed to Mary Smith, Dolby Estate, Lyndhurst.

"You're back Megs. How's your Mum?"

"We buried her two days ago. It may be a horrible thing to say but I'm glad she's out of it. Those mills are dreadful. So many of the workers being crippled with lung diseases."

"I'm so sorry." Mary put her arms around Meg and hugged her.

Megs untangled herself. "I'm all right, thanks Mary. A boy brought this for you."

"A boy? Who?"

"Dunno, Mary. Some wastrel said a man gave him the envelope and told him to deliver it to the kitchen here and he'd give him a shilling."

"Oh."

Megs hovered. Mary could tell she was itching to see who had written to her but she wasn't about to open it in company. Her imagination took off and instilled the idea that it could be from Johnny but then she remembered he knew her as Mary Dunsford not Mary

Smith so it couldn't be from him and why would it be? A handsome wealthy young soldier wouldn't correspond with a maid. She had never had a letter before. Her mind went into overdrive. There were several ne'er do wells in the village who thought she was ripe for plucking was the way she had heard them talk about her. Their ability to write she doubted. Curiosity clawed at her but she slipped the envelope into her dress pocket and carried on dead heading.

"You're not going to open it?"

"Later. I don't suppose it's important. Too busy just now. Thank you for bringing it."

"Maybe it's from that soldier."

"What soldier?"

"On the night of the ball. After you had been stood down by Mrs Williams, he came into the kitchen looking for you. I presume it was you because he described you. My he was a handsome ginger haired gentleman. He wanted to know the name of the maid he'd met in the dining room because he thought he knew her. I told him your name and that you'd gone off duty. He didn't say anything. Fancy a handsome soldier like that being interested in you. Oh my, sorry. I didn't mean it like that. I meant someone in his position and a maid. Oh, fiddlesticks I'd better shut up!"

"You didn't tell me."

"I left first thing next morning to see my Mum. Sorry but with all that going on I forgot. Is he your beau?"

"No. Just a case of mistaken identity I think."

"So, who is the letter from then?"

"Oh, probably one of those horrible men in the village."

Megs left; Mary could tell she was miffed. Such excitement for a maid to get a letter and Megs liked to know what was going on.

Her heart thumped in her chest. Johnny had recognised her. And that's why the letter was addressed to Mary Smith instead of Mary Dunsford she decided. Of course, that depended on whether the letter was indeed from Johnny.

Once alone Mary ripped open the letter.

"Dear Mary,

You have changed much since we parted all those years ago but I still remember the sparkle in your eyes and your smile. I'm sorry I didn't recognise you at first. By the time I realised who you were I could not find you though I looked throughout the house. A maid told me you had finished duty.

I could tell by the way you looked at me that you recognised me. I think I understand why you said we were not known to each other and the change of name.

We may meet again soon and I hope to have a proper conversation with you.

In case this letter is intercepted I shall say no more.

Your friend"

Mary stared at the letter unable to fathom what she thought. If Johnny had made inquiries, with whom other than Megs and what had been said? What did he know? She was supposed to be dead, drowned and maybe he knew that. The longing to see him fought with her need to protect herself. And when would she see him?

A quick glance over the letter again and then she put it back in her pocket just as Lady Eleanor came into the orangery.

"Hello, Mary. I need some cut flowers for a centre piece."

"Yes, Milady. Do you have any preference?"

"No, I'll leave that to you. They are for a centre piece for the table tonight. We're entertaining. Are you all right? You look a little flushed. I do hope you are not coming down with something. You've been working hard doing the two jobs. I'll speak to Mrs Williams and her husband to see if we can give you some time off."

"Er. . ., thank you Milady. It's a little warm in here, that's all."

"Splendid. I'll leave you to fill the vase. It's on the table in the dining room."

Mary took the vase from the dining room table. The butler and footman had already set the places with silver cutlery and crystal on a white tablecloth. It didn't take long to fill the vase with an array of blue flowers to match the blue napkins on the table. She had just finished placing it in the centre when Megs came in.

"Well, was the letter from your soldier?"

"He isn't my soldier."

"Hmmm. Well, tonight Cook says Lord Chegwidden's nephew is coming to dinner with two friends from his regiment. All three were here on the night of the ball so I expect one of them is the one asking about you."

"Oh!"

"I knew it! He's your beau!"

"No, but please don't say anything to anyone, Megs."

"My lips are sealed," said Megs pulling her forefinger across her lips. "But I'll want all the racy details after!"

"Megs! There will be no racy details."

"Aw! Lady Eleanor has invited the Reverend Postlethwaite, his wife and three daughters. Those girls are all eligible. You need to get in there quick with your soldier or one of them may trap him."

"What are you girls gossiping about? Get on with it," said Mr Templeton carrying an open bottle of red wine into the dining room and placing it next to a decanter.

"Just discussing the guest list for tonight Mr Templeton," said Megs breezing out of the door.

Chapter Thirteen

Mary sat on her bed holding the letter in her hand pondering what she should do. If Johnny was one of the soldiers coming to dinner how could she speak to him. Approaching a guest would be an infraction of the rules even in this enlightened household. And if the

Reverend's family were there, Johnny would not have the opportunity to find her. Mary wasn't on dinner duties so she wouldn't see him. *How can I get word to him?*

The hoped-for solution came in the guise of Megs. She was on dinner duty. Whether Megs would keep her mouth shut and not gossip was a risk but it was the only way Mary could think of seeing Johnny. She needed to know what he had discovered about her; that she was alleged to have stolen earrings, that she was convicted of a crime and that she was to be transported to Australia and that she had supposedly drowned. She need to speak to him to make sure he didn't accidentally give her away.

Mary found Megs picking sage in the herb garden for Cook. "Megs, could you do me a great favour? I will be forever in your debt if you do, please."

"Is it something to do with that soldier?"

"Yes, it is. I've written a note. Do you think you could give it to him without anyone seeing?"

"An assignation? Oh my. Where are you going to do it? In your rooms? Well, Mary, I reckon it's about time you lost it. I lost mine years ago."

"What? Oh! Megs! No. It's nothing like that."

"So you say! Yes, of course I'll give him your note. I've just got to have the details after, promise!"

"If there is anything to say I promise I will tell you Megs but you will be disappointed."

"You obviously don't know soldiers!"

Mary slipped a note from her pocket and placed it into Megs hand. She put it in her apron pouch. "Don't worry Mary I can keep a secret. You didn't tell on me when you found me in the hayloft with that sailor."

The night dragged as Mary lay unable to sleep wondering if Megs had managed to get the note to Johnny without being seen. She had watched the carriages arrive from her room and caught just a glimpse of Johnny's carrot top as he went up the steps into the house. He wore a frock coat instead of uniform. She also saw the Reverend and his family arrive. She'd seen the sisters at the church most Sundays and a little green worm of jealousy wriggled inside her for they were attractive and intelligent young ladies. Megs lived in the attic quarters and hadn't managed to get over to the stables after the dinner to give an update to her.

Sometime during the night, she managed to drop off to sleep and woke to a knocking on her door. The sun was up but it was Sunday and she didn't need to work. Today she would give church a miss and see if Johnny followed the invitation in the note to meet.

Her bare feet padded across the floorboards to the door.

"Mornin' Mary." Megs wore a huge grin. "Can I come in?"

Mary stood aside bursting with anticipation as Megs entered and sat on the side of the bed.

"Well?" Mary could hardly contain her excitement.

"I slipped it into his pocket and managed to whisper it was from you. He didn't react. My Mary, you've got a good 'un there. I noticed during the dinner that one of the sisters, Esme, showed a lot of interest in him."

"And he in her?"

Megs shook her head. "Nah! I don't think he was interested in her; I reckon he was interested in Catherine."

"Oh!

"Just joking Mary. My you've got it bad."

Mary wasn't sure she had 'got it bad' though he had kindled something inside her when she saw him in the dining room. The need to find out what he knew about her and whether he would turn her in was uppermost in her mind but she couldn't tell that to Megs. For now it was best if Megs thought she had a longing for Johnny and that was what it was all about.

***

After spending half an hour at the mirror checking how she looked in her Sunday best clothes and toying with her hair she was ready to see if Johnny would meet her.

The rendezvous was a fifteen-minute walk from Dolby House at the stone bridge near Bramble Farm. It would not appear out of place for a young woman to stand on the bridge and look down on the Beaulieu river to watch the fish, wildfowl, and flora. The added advantage of this place was the footpath that led into a wood where they could talk without being seen.

Sunshine and puffy clouds in the otherwise clear blue sky made for a pleasant stroll except for Mary it was a walk with butterflies in her tummy and clammy hands from wondering if he would come and if he did, what then?

While still a few minutes from the bridge she heard the distant church clock strike noon. That was the time she had put in the note. She hurried her steps and began to perspire so slowed down. Arriving in a sweaty condition was not the appearance she wanted to give and the thought of that reminded her that this meeting meant more to her than just finding out if Johnny was going to inform on her.

As she came round the bend there was the bridge and a tingle shot through her body.

Johnny stood looking down at the river.

"Mary!' he said with a huge smile as she approached.

"Johnny, thank you for coming. Can we go into the wood so we can talk without being seen?" She'd tried to deliver the question in a relaxed and confident manner but as soon as the words left her mouth, she knew they were full of excitement and anticipation.

"All right. You go ahead and I'll follow in a couple of minutes just in case someone should see us. Not that I mind of course but it may cause you a problem if we are seen together."

Mary climbed the style careful not to catch her dress on the post and set off along the gravel path for the wood fifty yards away. Once inside the wood she found a fallen oak tree and sat on the trunk.

A few minutes later Johnny arrived and sat beside her. "Well, Mary, I have to say this is a surprise. I heard you had drowned."

"Oh, so you know what I was accused of?"

"I saw it in the local newspaper. You were charged with stealing a pair of diamond earrings from Hartford House and sentenced to seven years transportation to Australia. It said you fell in the water while boarding the ship and drowned. It didn't say anything about a body being found but that was the presumption since you were in chains."

"That's just about it, Johnny. That's what happened but I managed to get out of the leg irons and swim to a fishing boat. From there people I didn't even know helped me. There are so many kind people in this world as well as bad ones."

"That's why you're calling yourself Mary Smith instead of Mary Dunsford?"

"Yes, if I'm found out I'll be sent to Australia probably for life as punishment for escaping."

"You are in constant danger then."

"Only if someone informs on me. Aren't you going to ask me if I stole the earrings?"

"After I saw you at the ball, I made some inquiries. The butler at Hartford House is the father of a sergeant in my company. He told me that you were wrongly convicted, that Lady Elizabeth gave you the earrings. Sir Edward has a reputation of getting what he wants from young women and the story is that you refused him so he arranged for you to be charged with stealing the earrings. Of course nobody can prove that but that is what most people at the estate believe. They won't say that in public, only in private because of the repercussions for them."

"So, the butler knows I'm still alive?"

"No. I just claimed to be interested in the case. I doubt he would have told me if he knew you were alive in case I dragged him into a court to give evidence, not that I could have done that anyway."

"You've done well for yourself Johnny. An officer in Queen Victoria's army."

"Yes. I'll inherit our estate at some time in the future but I wanted to see some of life away from there. The army gave me that opportunity."

"Why did you send the note, Johnny?"

"Mary, we were just children and I believe good friends. I liked you a lot but it was as a friend. Then when I saw you again at the ball after all those years, Mary, I'm not particularly good at this sort of thing. I'm embarrassed. Mary, I don't know, it was just something that made me want to see you again, to speak to you, to be your friend again. That's not entirely true, Mary, something happened to me when I saw you. I don't want to scare you but when I saw you my feelings were not of friendship. It was far more than that. I think I've made a fool of myself. Sorry for gibbering on."

Mary reached for his hand and held it to her bosom. "Johnny, that's so good to hear. But I'm a wanted felon and you are an officer in the army and from a good family. I don't think there is any future for us though I wish there were because I feel the same about you. My heart sang when I saw you in the dining room."

Chapter Fourteen

Mary sat in her room polishing her shoes. A knock at the door disturbed her thoughts of

Johnny.

"Hello Mary. Go on then. Tell me all about it. Did you sneak him in here? Did you do it? That's the fourth Sunday you've met him."

"Megs for goodness sake. We sat and chatted and that's all."

"Really! Oh! Are you going to meet him again?"

"Yes, next Sunday."

"C'mon. Something must have happened after four meetings. A soldier doesn't meet a young woman that many times and not try it on."

"He's a perfect gentleman, Megs."

"Huh! I've never met one of them."

"Well, he is. You won't tell on me?"

"Of course not. Any chance you can fix me up with one of his friends? Or one of his soldiers. I'm not fussy." Megs giggled making Mary laugh too.

"Megs! Maybe!"

"Anyway, I didn't come over here just to get the gory details. Mrs Williams sent me to ask you to come over to the house. Lady Eleanor requires your presence. Don't worry. You're not in trouble."

Mary put on her clean shoes, brushed herself down in the mirror and followed Megs over to the house where she found Angharad sitting in the kitchen.

"Ah, there you are Mary. Come with me. Lady Eleanor needs you."

Mary followed the housekeeper along the corridor to the drawing room. Lady Eleanor sat in a winged backed chair embroidering a flower that Mary recognised as an iris from its blue petals and long stem.

"Ah, Mary. Thank you for coming over. You know I haven't had a lady's maid since Jessica left. I thought I could manage with rotating the housemaids but I find myself being more and more required to assist my husband at social and business functions. So I need a lady's maid and after discussion with Mrs Williams I would like to offer the position to you."

This was undoubtedly a promotion. Butler, housekeeper, lady's maid was the hierarchy of the staff in service in Dolby House. But Mary wasn't sure. She would like to work for Lady Eleanor but her interest and love of gardening remained strong.

"Of course, I would still like you to be involved in the greenhouses and orangery. Your skill should not go to waste," said Lady Eleanor.

Mary beamed a reply. "Thank you, Milady. I would very much like to be your lady's maid."

"You are something of a mystery to us, Mary. I know little of where you came from or your previous employers. Not that it matters. You proved yourself to be honest, reliable and a good worker and that is what counts in my opinion. From your bearing and fine diction, I wondered if you were really someone from my social class perhaps hiding for a reason best known to yourself. Anyway, that's none of my business and I shall not interfere."

"Thank you, Milady." A tinge of guilt hovered around her inside at the thought of the trust her employer gave her.

Mary followed Angharad out of the drawing room, along the corridor and into her office where the housekeeper closed the door.

"Don't worry Mary. There is no likelihood of your past being discovered. And it was quite some time ago so I expect the authorities have lost interest since you are supposed to be dead."

"I can't tell you how grateful I am for everything you've done for me." Mary put her arms around her and gave her a hug.

"So, you start as lady's maid tomorrow. I'll tell Fred. He won't be happy at losing you but then he isn't really losing you because you'll still be working in the greenhouses and orangery."

***

Mary met Johnny at the usual time and place on Sunday and they headed for the wood and the tree trunk that had become their secret place.

Johnny seemed quieter than usual as they sat talking about her new job as lady's maid.

He seemed preoccupied. It began to worry Mary. "Is everything all right?"

Johnny nodded. "I don't want to upset you or alarm you but. . ."

Mary's tummy turned over. What was wrong? Would this be where he told her he couldn't meet her again?"

"Mary. . ." He took hold of her hand. "Mary, please forgive me if this offends you but. . . but may I kiss you?"

Mary blinked and felt a surge of relief that shyness troubled him not something more serious. This was their fifth meeting and they hadn't even held hands though she had wanted to from the first time they came into the wood.

"Yes."

He leaned forward. On her lips she felt his, at first as light as a feather and then a little stronger. With neither moving the kiss lasted for over two minutes. Mary pulled back only because she needed to take a breath though she didn't want to stop. Her cheeks turned the colour of roses in the greenhouse. Johnny's eyes fixed on hers, her beating heart and butterflies in her tummy told her she was in love. But it was a love that could never be. Not with her a lady's maid and him an eligible bachelor, soldier, and heir to a fortune. Mary would give up everything and happily live with him in penury but that could never be.

"What's wrong? I'm sorry if I was too forward," said Johnny taking hold of her hand.

"No, not at all. It's just that it seems so unfair. We can never be together; our backgrounds are too different. You couldn't be seen with me, a maid."

"That's how society works. We can continue to meet in secret if you don't mind."

"Johnny, of course I don't mind but how long will this go on for? We can't spend the rest of our lives seeing each other in the woods."

"I have some leave coming up. Do you think you could persuade Lady Elizabeth to let you take some time off and we could perhaps go somewhere and be together? Oh, I didn't mean to shock you. I'm sorry if that offends. I would not make any improper advances towards you er. . .beyond what you found acceptable."

Mary pondered for a moment. *What is he suggesting? Are we to go to some sordid seaside hotel and book in as man and wife where he would make love to me? I hope that's what he means.*

"Lady Elizabeth did say I could take some leave. I'll ask. Where would we go?"

"I visited Lyme Regis as a child. It's a pretty little town by the sea where nobody will know us."

***

Mary ran a comb with shaky hands through Lady Eleanor's auburn hair at the dressing table after laying out her clothes for the day on the bed.

"Whatever is the matter with you today, Mary?"

"Milady, you said after the ball that I may take some time off. I know that was a long time ago and I didn't want to take time off but would that be all right now?"

"Are you happy here, Mary? Is there anything wrong?"

"No, Milady, I'm mean no there is nothing wrong and yes I am happy here. It's just that I haven't had a holiday since. . . well ever. And I'd like to have one. I've saved up a little money and I think I would like to go somewhere by the sea."

"Mary, is there a young man involved in all this?"

"Er. . ." Mary couldn't lie. "Hmmm."

"Propriety Mary. Never forget propriety. Is it the young man you meet every Sunday?"

Mary's mouth fell open. Had Megs told on her? "Er. . ."

"I'd like to meet this young man. I've seen you slipping off every Sunday at the same time and that in my opinion can only mean one thing. I do hope he is a respectable young man."

"He is, Milady. That's the problem. He's not of my class, he's your class."

"Going with a young man to the seaside or wherever you are planning, that seems somewhat risky and is likely to lead to one thing. Is marriage on the cards?"

"Er. . .I don't see how it can be."

"No, I don't suppose it is. Oh dear Mary. I do hope you don't get your heart broken. Is this young man taking advantage of you?"

"Er. . .not yet."

"Hmmm, I didn't mean that. Is he using his position to put undue pressure on you to comply with what are probably his intentions?"

"No, no, Milady. He's only kissed me once."

"Breathe not a word of what I am going to tell you, but I shall reveal something about myself that will show you I am not a stuffy upper-class shallow woman and I understand the quandary that you find yourself in. Twenty-three years ago, when I was nineteen, I met a handsome sailor, an officer on HMS Beagle. Not one born into the class, he had worked his way up from the lower decks so you will appreciate that socially he was not acceptable to my father. Have you heard of that ship?"

"Yes, I read Mr Darwin's book about his voyage. Mr Williams gave it to me to read because there's a lot of information in it about tropical places and he knew I was interested in such things."

"This young sailor and I went to a small village on the Welsh coast where we would not be known. We had a wonderful week. He sailed two weeks later for the voyage that should have been for two years but took five. While he was away, I married Lord Chegwidden as our families had arranged it. I never saw my sailor again."

"Oh!"

"Our love could never be. But don't be sad for me because this life is what I am born into and my husband is a good man. I've told you this story so you will know that your relationship is probably doomed. You do understand that? If he is of my class his parents will already have chosen a wife for him."

"Yes, I do understand. Am I wicked to want to spend some time with him?"

"No, of course not. Another thing you need to learn about life, Mary, is that so-called respectable men can get away with bedding as many women they can seduce while respectable women are required to be the epitome of chastity for their husbands. I hope it is not like that forever. Arrange your holiday with your beau and then come back to me. I only hope he is a good man."

"Thank you, Milady." Mary's eyes widened as a smile crossed her lips. This woman for whom she was a maid had suddenly grown in stature. Underneath she was a woman just like Mary.

Chapter Fifteen

Mary climbed down from the railway carriage at Dorchester station with her carpet bag in one hand. She jumped in fright when the locomotive disgorged a jet of steam into the air.

Johnny, still chuckling at her reaction to the steam took her bag and with his bag in his other hand they weaved their way through the crowd on the platform.

Once outside Johnny put the bags on the roadside. "I'll find a carriage."

She watched him stroll along the road. A tinge of excitement ran through her body. He looked so handsome in his frock coat and top hat. He would have looked even better in his uniform but that would just draw attention to them and they wanted to be as inconspicuous as possible.

The street bustled with activity with horses and carts, carriages, costermongers calling their wares and people on horseback.

A black roofed cab pulled by two huge horses came to a stop in front of her. Johnny opened the door and stepped down. Up on the driver's seat a man in a heavy black coat with white piping around the edges lifted his top hat to her.

"This is our transport. The driver thinks it will take around three to four hours to Lyme Regis."

Mary stroked the nearest horse's head. A tattoo on its side attracted her attention.

"What's that?" she asked the driver.

"Used to be Artillery horses. Bought them when they retired," said the driver in a deep west country voice.

Johnny handed her up to the cab. Inside she looked around at the plush interior. Two red leather bench seats and padded walls was a clear indication to Mary that this was an expensive way to travel. She was no stranger to riding in upper-class carriages since taking the role of Lady's made first with Lady Elizabeth at Hartford House and now at Dolby House with Lady Eleanor. But this was the first time that she was one of the principal passengers and she liked it.

Johnny threw their bags up to the driver who stored them on the roof. "Is this all right?" said Johnny as he climbed in and sat down beside her.

"Oh yes."

The carriage set off. At first it made slow progress through the streets of Dorchester until they were out on the open road. Mary sat with her hands clasped in her lap trying to keep the butterflies in her tummy still.

Occasional bumps in the road shook the carriage as it thundered through the countryside. Suddenly it stopped.

Johnny put his head out of the window. "What's happening?" "Out," said a voice.

Mary could hear another voice. "Get out and don't try anything."

Johnny turned to Mary. "Highwaymen. Keep calm and don't worry. They're only after money. It isn't worth risking anything just for money. Stay by my side."

He opened the door, stepped out and then offered his hand to Mary. She took it and stepped down. Two men with masks over their mouths and noses on horseback held pistols. One pointed at Johnny and one at the driver.

"Pretty young thing," said one of the highwaymen."

"Hmmm. She may have to be the prize unless there's rich pickings."

Johnny twitched. These men meant ill intent for her but what could he do to protect her? They were armed, Johnny was not. Or was he, she wondered? When she was thrown against him on the bumpy road, something hard on his side dug into her. His frock coat was long enough to cover a pistol, she hoped.

"When I say jump, jump behind me," whispered Johnny.

"What did you say?" said one of the highwaymen. "Empty your pockets, now."

"Jump," said Johnny.

Mary jumped behind him.

Johnny drew a short-barreled revolver from under his frock coat. Two massive bangs rent Mary's ears. Neither hit the highwaymen. A third shot came from one of the robbers. Johnny lurched backwards holding his shoulder. He dropped his pistol and collapsed to the ground.

The driver struck at a highwayman with his whip but missed. The man fired at him but he missed. Jumping from the driver's seat on the far side of the carriage from the robbers the driver let out a scream as he hit the ground and writhed holding his leg.

The horses whinnied but did not bolt, perhaps gunfire from the army days accustomed them to the noise.

Mary grabbed Johnny's pistol and pointed it at the robbers with her finger trembling on the trigger. For moment there was a stand-off as the robbers pointed their guns at Mary and she pointed hers at them. Suddenly they turned their horses and galloped away.

Johnny moaned.

She helped him sit up against the coach's back wheel and undid his coat. A red patch spread over his shoulder. With shaking hands, she ripped off his cravat, tore his shirt and stuffed the cravat into the wound. Johnny moaned, only semi-conscious.

Satisfied the cravat stopped the bleeding she hurried over to the coach driver. He was alive but his leg bent at a crazy angle.

"I'll have to get you both to a doctor."

"I can't drive the carriage."

"I can."

Mary helped Johnny up the step and into a seat. She checked the cravat in his shoulder. It still held back the blood.

With a supreme effort from her and profanity from the driver, she helped him into the carriage next to Johnny

Up on the driver's seat Mary tapped the flanks of the horses with the whip. Off they trotted.

***

The coach pulled into a small town on the turnpike. Mary didn't know the name of it. The sight of a young woman with bloodstains on her coat attracted attention including the attention of a constable, the last thing she wanted.

"What's happenin' Miss?" called the Constable as Mary brought the horses to a halt.

"Highwaymen out on the road. They shot my friend. He's inside with the driver who has a broken leg. Is there a doctor in the town?"

"Maisie!" called the constable to a woman standing outside a haberdashery. "Go fetch

Doc Pilkington."

Mary climbed down from the coach and opened the door. Johnny lay prone on the seat but she could see he was still breathing and when he smiled, with a twinge in his now pale face, relief flooded through her entire body.

A mouthful of profanities came from the driver.

"Mind your language," said the Constable. "How far out did this happen, Miss?"

"About three or four miles."

"And you managed to get away? Which way did the robbers go?"

"I don't know."

Chapter Sixteen

Mary sat in the doctor's surgery while the medic bandaged Johnny's shoulder. "Not too bad," said the Doctor. "Lucky no bones hit. You've lost some blood, not as bad as it looks, so you must rest for a few weeks."

Mary put her hand on his uninjured shoulder. "I'll take you back home and you can recuperate there. I don't think we can go on to where we were going."

"No, I don't suppose we can."

A knock at the door made Mary jump. Keeping her hands from trembling since the incident on the road had been difficult though she believed nobody would expect less in the circumstances.

The Constable came in. "My sergeant is here. He needs to speak with you Miss for the report. And you too sir if you are ready."

This was something Mary had expected and dreaded. "Of course, Constable. When would he like to speak to me?"

"Now if that is convenient Miss."

"Perhaps he could see us both at the same time, Constable," said Johnny.

"I'll ask him." The constable left.

"I'll leave you two alone for a few minutes. After your ordeals you may need some time together quietly." The doctor gathered up his instruments and left the room.

"They will want to know where we were going and why."

"Mary, I expect the sergeant is a man of the world. A wealthy young soldier travelling with a young woman to whom he isn't married. He'll know what we were doing. It isn't against the law, well not the legal one, maybe the moral one but that isn't punishable in this life."

Mary looked at Johnny trying to fathom what she meant to him and concluded that it was everything.

***

Mary knocked on the drawing room door.

"Come in," came a voice from inside.

Mary entered and curtsied to Lady Eleanor.

"Well, my dear, what a pickle you managed to fall into. I'm all in favour of a young woman having an adventure but I did not expect this. "

Mary didn't know what to say so she didn't say anything.

"Come and sit down, Mary." She pointed at the sofa opposite her winged backed chair.

Mary wasn't usually invited to sit down in the presence of her employer and the instruction began to make her tummy turn over. Was she about to be dismissed?

"Thank you for your honesty in telling me about what happened. You haven't named the young man and I do not need to know. I am pleased that you say he is an honest and upright person. You were both incredibly lucky to survive. From what you told me the young man will make a full recovery, thank the Good Lord."

"Yes, Milady. Will you dismiss me?"

"I do not intend to dispense with your services. My husband left the matter in my hands. I do believe you should think carefully about this relationship but I shall not interfere."

"Thank you, Milady."

After the sun went down and she lay on the bed in the darkness, a knock at the door made her sit up. "Who is it?"

"Megs."

"Come in."

Megs came in and sat on the bed next to Mary and took her hand in hers. "Well, such excitement. Anyway, your beau sent you a note." She reached into her apron and produced an envelope and a lucifer. She lit a candle on the bedside table and then sat down and waited for Mary to open the envelope.

Mary took a deep breath and ran her forefinger over the envelope flap.

"Dear Mary,

This is dreadful. I had to pretend that our trip was nothing more than me taking advantage of my position to have a debauched week with a young maid. Had I not done so, my father would have taken the time to investigate who you are and I could not allow that to happen for the obvious reason. He is in favour of me sowing my wild oats as they call it but would not have countenanced a serious relationship between you and me.

I care not one jot for what he may do to me if he realised that I love you. It is what would happen to you that fills me with worry. Even if he didn't discover your identity, he would undoubtedly disinherit me though I do not care. My future lies with you, and I hope you feel the same.

Until I manage to find a way forward where we can be together without my father digging into your past, we must be careful and avoid seeing each other.

You can be assured that when I can, I will come for you and we will stay together.

I sincerely hope that I have not overestimated your feelings for me. I need to know if you love me and if you do then I will move whatever mountain needs moving to get us together.

If you want me, I will be yours forever as your husband. And if you do, please leave a note under our tree trunk on Sunday 9th October which I know is two weeks away but I won't be able to collect it until then. I will pick it up the following day to make sure I am not seen with you. If there is no note then I will know that I have made a grave mistake for which I apologise and I give you my word that I will never bother you again.

My undying love

Johnny

PS The doctor says I will be fine in a couple of weeks if I rest the wound."

Mary clasped the note to her chest and burst into joyful tears.

"Can I read it?" said a hopeful Megs.

"Certainly not!"

***

Saturday night dragged by as Mary lay in her bed. She had gone over and over in her mind what she should write. There was no doubting her feelings for Johnny and she wanted to be with him. He wanted to marry her. If he could arrange it somehow, she would.

When the sun came up, she stepped out of bed, took a pencil and a piece of paper that she had taken from Lady Eleanor's desk and began to write what she had troubled over all night.

"Dear Johnny,

Your note has given me hope. I understand that we must be careful so that in the future we can be together when you can find a way that will not result in your father researching my past.

I love you Johnny and I accept your proposal of marriage.

However long it takes, I will wait for you.

With all my love

Mary"

She slipped the note into an envelope, sealed it, and put it in her coat pocket. This was her day off. She didn't need to wait until the usual meeting time of noon with Johnny because he wouldn't be there. With a skip in her step, she came down the stairs and out into the stable yard where she met Angharad heading her way in a tizzy.

The Brougham carriage stood outside the stable with two grooms harnessing Belle the chestnut mare.

"Where are you going? I was just coming over to fetch you," said Angharad, red in the face.

"Just for a walk. I need some fresh air. What's happening?"

"Never mind that now. Come with me. Lady Eleanor's mother has had an accident, she's badly hurt. Milady is off to Oxford this morning to see what she needs and wants you with her to help. Come with me."

Mary felt the envelope in her pocket. She needed to put it under the tree trunk for Johnny to find. Maybe, she hoped, she could slip away for half an hour before they departed for Oxford. She hung her coat by the back door and slipped the envelope into her dress pocket.

Lady Eleanor sat at her dressing table in her nightdress brushing her hair when Mary knocked and entered.

"Oh splendid, Mary. Please pack some day clothes for me and I think I shall only need two evening wear dresses as I doubt we will be doing much entertaining."

Mary lifted down a large leather suitcase from the shelf in the bedroom closet. Lady Eleanor usually travelled with a trunk of clothes but Mary could see her mind was on getting to Oxford as quickly as possible. Even so, she was unable to put all that her employer wanted in one case so she went to the storeroom in the attic to find another and Megs.

To her great relief she found Megs still in bed. It was her day off too and the panic downstairs had so far not involved her.

"What's all the noise downstairs and outside?" said Megs when Mary knocked on her door and went in.

"Lady Eleanor's mother has had a serious accident. We must go to Oxford now. Megs, I need you to do something for me without telling anyone. Will you do it for me?"

"Does this involve that gorgeous beau of yours?"

"Yes."

"Oh my Mary. I thought that was all over. Well, well. What do you want?"

"I need you to put an envelope under a certain tree trunk. Make sure you push it under in case it rains. I need you to do that today. Will you, please Megs?"

"Yes. Where's the tree trunk?"

"You know the path with a stile near the bridge on the edge of the estate, it leads to a wood?"

"Yes, I passed it often enough though I've never been down the path. I say, is that where you and your fella used to do it?"

"Megs, we didn't 'do it'. It's where we used to meet. Where the path leads into the wood, off to the right there's a fallen oak tree. Slip this envelope under the centre of the tree today before dark. That's especially important, Megs."

"All right. Understood. In the wood off to the right, fallen oak tree, centre, put the envelope under. Got it."

"You're an angel, Megs."

"I hope not and I still want the racy details!"

Chapter Seventeen

Lady Bicester lay in her four-poster bed with her daughter Eleanor by her side on a Queen Anne red upholstered chair. The old woman's breathing was shallow and laboured.

Mary brought in a tray with two bowls of soup. "Cook sent this up for you Milady. Should I try to feed your mother?"

"No Mary. Let her rest. I think she is beyond food now. And I'm afraid I'm not hungry, you have it. Sit over there by the table. You've been so helpful to us these last four weeks and I don't know how I can thank you."

Mary sat at the mahogany table and spooned a mouthful of chicken broth. The weeks were sad with the old lady who had steadily deteriorated after falling downstairs at this vast stately home in the Oxfordshire countryside. Though she had her own staff, Mary had taken on most of the work for the old lady at the behest of Lady Eleanor.

Suddenly there was silence and then a cry. Mary jumped to her feet; tears fell from her employer's puffy eyes as she held her mother's hand. That the old woman had passed was clear to Mary. Without thinking or remembering her place she stepped over to Lady Eleanor and put her arm around her shoulder. "I'm so sorry."

***

Lady Eleanor, her husband and members of their social class stood around the graveside in the light drizzle while Mary, other servants and local people stood further back to watch the gravediggers lower a coffin into the ground. The rotund vicar intoned words that Mary didn't follow as her mind was on getting back to Dolby House to discover if Johnny had found a way for them to be together, safely.

***

Mary felt butterflies in her tummy as the brougham pulled into the Dolby stable yard six weeks after it left. The ride from Oxford was not as comfortable as the ride there since she had to travel in the open next to the driver as Lord Chegwidden was with his wife inside.

She couldn't wait to find Megs to discover if any word had arrived from Johnny in answer to her note.

Two grooms and a footman appeared as if from nowhere and between them and Mary they unhitched the horse and unloaded the baggage while Lord Chegwidden escorted his wife inside.

Mary unpacked Lady Eleanor's clothes, some to the closet and some to the laundry and then set off to find Megs. She found her friend in the pantry filling jars with Cook's jam from a copper pot and made a quick check around to ensure that she and Megs were alone.

"Any word from you know who?"

"No."

"You did leave the envelope?"

"Yes, where you told me."

"I thought he would have made contact. I must try to contact him but how?"

"Can't you write to him?"

"At home? No. The letter may be intercepted and I don't want his father to find it?"

"I don't understand Mary. Why are you so afraid of your relationship coming out? It's out already although I suppose his parents don't know who exactly he was dallying with. It isn't unusual for a man of his standing to have a girl from the lower classes if it doesn't involve the girl trying to climb above her social place. I doubt his parents would care that he was. . . you know. . .you."

"He isn't, you know, me. Can we leave it at that?"

"All right, all right. Don't get your drawers in a twist. Look, why don't you go to the barracks. I'm sure none of the soldiers will be concerned that he's. . . sorry, concerned about you and him."

"Megs, that's a brilliant idea. Sorry for being a grump. Thanks."

"I'll come with you next Sunday if you like. Might find myself a soldier boy."

"His barracks are near Winchester. I think we can go there by train."

***

Sunday morning came after what seemed the longest week in Mary's life. With Megs she set off by coach and train on a sunny morning after raiding her piggy bank for the fares.

In a compartment they had to themselves Mary looked out of the window trying to keep her excitement under control.

"So, how are you going to do this, Mary? Are we going to turn up at the gate and ask for him?"

"How else can we do it?"

"Dunno. I suppose that's the only way."

A short coach ride from the station took them to the barracks in the countryside near Winchester. Two soldiers in red jackets and rifles over their shoulders stood guard at a gate.

"Hello," said Mary unsure how one should address a guard.

"Hello," smiled one of the soldiers with a look up and down, a look that Mary recognised had thoughts behind it.

"I need to see Lieutenant John Sandes."

The soldier grinned but stayed with his rifle over his shoulder. "Lieutenant Sandes? He's a Hussar, isn't he?"

"Yes."

"That regiment's gone. Three weeks ago."

"Gone? Gone where?"

"Crimea."

"Where's that? Is it up north?"

"Don't you know anything?"

Mary turned to Megs. Megs shrugged.

"What do you mean?" said Mary.

"Don't you read the newspapers?" said the soldier.

"When would I have time to read newspapers?"

"The Russians. The army's gone off to fight the Ruskies in the Crimea. It's somewhere near Turkey."

"Turkey? Oh my God, I know where that is. When are they are coming back?"

"When they've finished with the Russians. Miss, I don't have a bloody clue but I'm off duty in two hours if you and your friend want to meet me and mine down at The Pheasant for a drink."

"Yeah," said Megs.

"No," said Mary. "We have to get back." She took Megs by the elbow and hurried her away from the gate. "Now what do I do. I can't understand why he hasn't left word that he was going. Perhaps he knew I was away and didn't want to leave a note at Dolby like he has done before. I don't know why. Perhaps he left one under the oak tree."

Much to Megs annoyance that she was deprived from having a drink with the soldiers, the two of them headed back to Dolby via the wood.

Mary searched all over the tree trunk but did not find any envelope or note. She sat down on the trunk and held back her tears before noticing that Megs had a worried expression on her face.

"What's wrong?"

"Er, Mary, don't get mad but. . . but is this the tree?"

"What do you mean? Of course this is the tree. What? Oh no!"

"I'm so sorry."

"Where did you put it?" Mary jumped to her feet.

Megs took her further along the path to another fallen oak tree, reached under it, and pulled out a soggy envelope.

Mary fell to her knees and sobbed.

"I'm so sorry, Mary. But he'll be back and he'll come for you."

No, he won't. His note said if he didn't hear from me then he would know I don't love him and he will never bother me again. I've lost him, Megs."

"Mary!" Megs fell to her knees, burst into tears, and put her arms around her friend's legs.

Chapter Eighteen

The weeks dragged by. At every opportunity Mary read
the reports on the progress of the Crimea campaign by
William Howard Russell in the London Times that Lord
Chegwidden would leave in the breakfast room.

On a miserable 1854 autumn morning after his lordship
had finished his devilled kidneys and retired to smoke in
the conservatory, she picked up that morning's Times.
Inside as she turned the pages, she stopped to read about a
battle near a place called Balaclava. Her heart thumped as
the story of six hundred men including the Hussars
charged the Russian guns. The way the battle unfolded in
the newspaper was one of glory with heavy casualties but
Mary felt deep inside that what was written was a gloss
over a terrible loss of British soldiers. Her mind tried to
expunge any thought that one of those lives lost could be
Johnny.

The days passed and each day she read the newspaper for
more information about the war in the Crimea.

Lady Eleanor came into the breakfast room and found
Mary sitting in a chair with the newspaper.

"Oh, I didn't realise you were interested in the
news. What are your reading?" "Sorry Milady. I
was just tidying up." Mary jumped to her feet.

"It's all right Mary. I don't mind. I like that you are taking
an interest in what is in the news. Anything interesting?"

"I was reading about the war in the Crimea, Milady."

"Oh, yes. Dreadful. According to my husband there was an awful disaster when the

British charged the Russian guns. It appears that they are saying it was a glorious act of British heroism when they charged. He says it was a huge mistake. Anyway, that is for the people in government to worry about. I must impose on you to step in again for a dinner tonight. We have eighteen coming. Lord Chegwidden is putting together a project to help

Nurse Nightingale with funding her new ideas to help our soldiers in hospitals in the Crimea.

I don't know some of the guests but provided they donate money to the cause they are welcome."

"Oh, that's such a marvellous idea. I'll be pleased to help, Ma'am."

***

Mary hurried across the damp stable yard dressed in a long black dress, white apron, and white lace cap to help with serving at table. She found Angharad in her usual calm giving out orders to the scullery maids, footmen, and Megs. Even the three chambermaids had been pressed into service for this big night.

"Ah here you are Mary," said Cook. "Milady wants you and Megs to serve the people at the top of the table. That's his lordship, two ladies and two gentlemen. Now, does everyone know what they are doing?"

"Yes," filled the kitchen.

Under the professional guidance of Angharad and Mr Templeton, Cook laid out the first course of turtle soup for the servers to carry to table.

Mary, adept at serving at table, carried three bowls and served his lordship, the elderly woman to his left and a distinguished middle-aged gentleman in Royal Navy uniform next to her. Megs managed two bowls and served the younger woman to his lordship's right and fiftyish gentleman in white tie and tails.

As she placed the bowl in front of the naval officer, she looked across the table. Her heart missed a beat. Years had passed since she left Hartford House, she had blossomed into a young woman from the sixteen-year-old girl she was then. Would he recognise her? How could she ever forget Sir Edward Glendenning? He hadn't changed at all. And then their eyes met but did he recognise her? She didn't know. Perhaps, she hoped, the snake just thought her attractive. After all, many maids must have passed through his hands, some literally since that dreadful day. Why would he remember just one of them and to the world Mary Dunsford was dead, she was Mary Smith.

The second course was filet of sole. Mary managed to keep her fears under control and as she served, she kept her head to one side in the hope that Glendenning wouldn't see her face too often and remember her.

During the next course of lamb chops shown on the menu as '*Cotelettes d'Agneau en Belle-Vue*' she risked a look across the table at Glendenning. He smiled at her.

The courses kept coming. Even though fear was a constant companion during the serving she wondered how the ladies in their tight corsets managed to get through so much food in one sitting.

By the fifth course Mary saw Glendenning was extremely interested in her. Still, she hoped it was his libido not his memory that created the interest. She knew she could handle the former but not the latter.

Eventually and much to her relief the dinner finished, the ladies repaired to the drawing room while the gentlemen had their cigars and port.

Mary helped the scullery maids though she was very tired. She didn't want to go back to her rooms over the stables and be alone if Glendenning had managed to elicit where she slept and wanted to pursue what he failed to obtain all those years ago.

Mr Templeton came into the kitchen and addressed the staff. "Well, I am pleased to pass on the compliments of his lordship and Lady Eleanor on your excellent and professional work tonight. It appears they raised a substantial amount to help Nurse Nightingale. Well done. And I would like to add my thanks to you all for your efforts tonight."

The staff drifted away to their quarters leaving Mary and Mr Templeton alone in the kitchen. He poured himself a cognac but didn't offer one to Mary.

"Have all the guests gone, Mr Templeton?"

"Yes, Mary. Off you go to bed now and I'll see you tomorrow."

Mary hurried across the yard to the stables with her eyes darting all around in case Glendenning should be lurking in the shadows. Once in her room she bolted the door and put a chair under the handle. Only then did she relax. She had got away with it. Glendenning's interest in her was carnal and not a memory.

Though much relieved to have made it through the dinner, sleep came slowly.

***

Two days after the trauma of seeing Sir Edward a trip out on the Solent aboard Lord

Chegwidden's yacht came as welcome distraction.

Mary carried a picnic basket aboard the gaff rigged ketch and put it in the bow. The only crew was his lordship's trusty old skipper Sam. Expecting it to be cool at sea, she had a coat that she put on a seat ready for later. For now, she was warm enough in her light summer dress that Lady Eleanor had loaned her. It wasn't one of her best but it was clearly good quality and not what Mary would usually wear. On the wooden deck she kicked off her ankle boots and went barefoot with permission from Lady Eleanor who followed suit.

By the time they were loaded and on their way the sun was high shining on the white Needles rocks. Mary sat in the bow still fretting about Sir Edward but enjoying the feel of the salty air on her face as the ketch cut through the gentle swell. Lady Eleanor and her husband sat each side of the centre beam in light conversation while Sam stood at the tiller.

Mary wondered if Johnny liked to sail. They had never discussed it. Almost a year had passed since she last saw him. A return visit to the barracks failed to obtain when Johnny's regiment would come home.

"I think we'll have the picnic now," said Lady Eleanor.

Mary lifted the basket to the centre ducking under the boom as she set a table with Cook's assortment of pies, chicken drumsticks. sandwiches, sausages, and cakes.

"Too much here for us," said Lady Eleanor. "Sam, Mary you will have to help us. Mary fill a plate for Sam please and then join us at the table."

Mary felt embarrassed. She'd never sat down to a meal with Lady Eleanor and had hardly spoken to his lordship though he always gave her a friendly greeting when they met in the mornings. He was nothing like Sir Edward. All the staff liked Lord Chegwidden even though he seemed somewhat aloof.

She filled a plate and took it aft to Sam who wasted no time in tucking into his lunch.

Mary returned to the table. Lord Chegwidden sat on the port side and Lady Eleanor opposite. Mary used the picnic basket on its side as a seat.

As she munched on a ham sandwich, Mary was careful to eat with the good manners that Mr Stevens at Hartford House had taught her. It helped her to follow Lady Eleanor's approach to the picnic. For a fleeting moment she daydreamed that she was here on the yacht with Lord and Lady Chegwidden and she was their daughter.

"I'll check if the wine is cooled," said Lord Chegwidden. He stepped towards the stern, leaned over the side, pulled on a rope, and brought a bottle of white wine out of the sea where it was chilling. As he stood straight the sail caught a sudden gust and swung the boom towards him.

Though he tried to duck it hit him on the forehead and knocked him overboard.

Lady Eleanor screamed.

Sam held on to the tiller and tried to bring the boat around but he couldn't do it directly. Even though Mary was not a sailor she guessed that turning a yacht under sail would be a difficult manoeuvre.

Lady Eleanor held on tight to the gunwale looking out at her husband now a few yards behind the yacht and floating face downwards.

Splash. Mary hit the cold water. It sucked the breath from her and brought back memories of her escape from the convict ship. She powered through the water to the body of Lord Chegwidden. With an effort she managed to turn him over so his head was out of the water. A glance at the yacht told her the distance was lengthening and getting further away on a wide circle to turn back. The shore looked nearer. With her arm around the unconscious peer, she swam for a beach where a group of people sat. One of the group stood and waded out into the sea but he was too far inshore to help her. She continued to swim towards him, kicking hard with her legs and paddling with her free arm.

Exhausted she ploughed on and managed to reach the man standing in the water. He helped her drag Lord Chegwidden ashore.

"I'm a doctor," said the man. "Turn him on his front."

She panted. Unable to stand she stayed down and tried to help turn him over.

Mary now saw the group was a family having a picnic. The wife ran over to them and helped the doctor and her turn Lord Chegwidden over. The doctor began to press down on his back in a pumping action. Lord Chegwidden brought up water, coughed and then began to gulp in deep breaths. The doctor helped him to sit up.

Mary slumped back to the beach and lay there looking at the blue sky. Death for her and his lordship had come close but she had chased it away.

Quite some time elapsed before the yacht ran aground on the beach. Lady Eleanor jumped from the boat and threw her arms around her husband who still sat on the sand taking in breaths.

"Mary saved my life."

Lady Eleanor let go of her husband and hugged Mary. "Thank you. Thank you, Mary," she said through her tears of relief.

Chapter Nineteen

Since the rescue of his lordship from drowning Mary
found herself the talk of the estate. Lord Chegwidden
seemed less aloof and his attitude to Mary became
avuncular without any underlying tone or motive that she
had encountered with Sir Edward. The worry that Sir
Edward may have recognised her still lingered.

Another week went by with Mary checking the newspaper
every morning for information about the war. Her worries
about Glendenning began to fade as her worries about
Johnny increased. When he made it back home, if he made
it back home, she would throw all caution to the wind and
approach him to tell him that she loved him and about the
mistake Megs made with the letter. How she would
discover when he had returned, she had not yet worked out
but she determined to do so. The barracks seemed the best
route though he may return to a different base.

Mary brushed Lady Eleanor's hair in front of the dressing
table mirror after breakfast ready for her ladyship's
morning appointment with the local vicar. A knock at the
door interrupted the coiffure.

"Come in," called Lady Eleanor.

Megs stood in the open doorway. "Ma'am, his Lordship asks that you join him in the drawing room as soon as possible. There's a sergeant and a constable with him."

Mary dropped the hairbrush.

"Oh! Let's hope they've caught the culprit who set fire to the old barn. Why he needs me I have no idea. All right. Tell him I shall be down in five minutes."

Megs closed the door. Mary heard her footsteps on the corridor. Everything around her seemed at a heightened level. The breathing of her ladyship, her own breathing, the dust particles in the air seemed to hang still.

"I'll wear the pale blue dress today, Mary."

Mary walked into the closet and brought out a burgundy dress.

"Mary, wake up! I said the blue dress."

"Sorry Milady."

Dressed in her blue dress, Lady Eleanor left Mary in the bedroom.

Mary ran through her options. They were few. She could jump out of the window but it was a long way down and she may break her leg. If she didn't, what could she do then? She could hide somewhere but they would find her. Then she sucked in a deep breath. If Glendenning had recognised her, he would have sent the police before now. Stop worrying, she told herself. Lady Eleanor said it was about the barn fire.

One carful step at a time and still with her blood singing in her ears, Mary descended the back stairs to the kitchen where she found Angharad, alone.

"I'm worried. The police are here. Do you know why?" said Mary.

"No." Angharad shook her head. "Mr Templeton let them in. He said there was a gentleman with them but he didn't say who."

"My previous employer was at the dinner last week and he seemed to show an interest in me."

"What? I didn't have a guest list, just numbers of men and women. If I knew Sir Edward was among them, I never would have sent you out there. Do you think he recognised you?"

"I don't know. He showed interest but that could be for other reasons."

"Yes, you're a pretty girl and he has a reputation. I'll see what I can discover. Wait here."

Angharad rushed out of the kitchen. Mary noticed how the always calm housekeeper seemed flustered adding to her own concern. She resolved to ensure that if the police were here for her she would not implicate Angharad in helping her.

Megs came in. "Blimey Mary, you look like you've seen a ghost."

"Maybe you're looking at one."

"What? What're talking about?"

Angharad came into the kitchen. "Mary, please come with me."

From the expression on Angharad's face she could tell all was not well. Resignation took hold.

***

The tall figure of Lord Chegwidden stood by the fireplace in the drawing room while Lady Eleanor sat in a winged back chair. A uniformed police officer and one with a bowler hat under his arm stood next to his lordship. Sergeant Phillips looked greyer but there was doubt it was him and when Mary's eyes fell on Sir Edward leaning on the back of the sofa with a smirk, she knew the game was up.

"Yes, that's her," said Sir Edward Glendenning pointing at Mary.

"I can't believe it," said Lady Eleanor. "Mary is the best lady's maid I have ever had. She is as honest as the day is long. I will not hear of such nonsense."

"She's not only honest, but she's also the bravest of the brave. Mary saved my life by risking her own when I nearly drowned," said Lord Chegwidden.

"Hmmm," coughed Phillips.

"Go ahead, officer, but I'm sure this all a mistake," said Lord Chegwidden.

"Hello again Miss Dunsford. You were believed to have drowned while boarding a convict transportation vessel in Portsmouth harbour. Do you have anything to say about that?"

Angharad stood by Mary's side. Mary heard her take in a breath to speak up If she defended Mary, then she too could be in serious trouble. After all the help she had given her it was something she could not countenance.

"I lied my way into employment here. Nobody here knows who I am."

Lady Eleanor pulled a lace handkerchief from her sleeve and dabbed her eyes. "No. No. I don't believe it. And if

161

she is who she says she is, I am sure there was a miscarriage of justice. I will make sure she had the best legal defence in the country."

"Well, are you going to arrest this woman?" demanded Sir Edward. "I told you more than a week ago about her and it's taken you all this time to come for her. Get on with it man or I'll speak to the Chief Constable. He's a member of my club."

"Sit down!" said Phillips in such a loud voice as he pointed at Sir Edward that everyone in the room jumped in surprise. "The reason it has taken me over a week to come here is because I have made inquiries. It always worried me about the allegation you made but I found no evidence to counter your allegation. And then I learned Miss Dunsford had drowned so there was nothing more I could do. I made it my business to come to your house when I learned of your allegation that Miss Dunsford was still alive."

"Where is this going? I demand you arrest Dunsford this minute. I'm warning you; I'll have you dismissed from the force."

Phillips sniffed. "After I left your house, Sir Edward, two of your staff came to me. On their consciences for years, they carried a burden. You threatened them with violence and unemployment if they admitted they knew that your late wife had given a pair of diamond earrings to Miss Dunsford. So they did not come forward at the time. When they discovered that Miss Dunsford was still alive and you had reported her to the police, they decided to tell the truth."

"Who, which members of my staff? I'll have them whipped! It's lie. She's a thief. Do your duty man!" bellowed Sir Edward still standing.

"They suggested I made inquiries about the death of your wife too. There are questions you will have to answer regarding that because I saw her doctor. Due to his conscience bothering him he made a statement. It can be a terrible companion can conscience, sir."

Phillips nodded to the Constable.

"I am arresting you for perjury and on suspicion of murder," said the Constable in a calm deep voice. He took a pair of handcuffs from his pocket and reached for Sir Edward's arm.

Sir Edward shoved the officer and stepped aside, strode forward, and grabbed Mary round the neck twisting her so that her body was between him and the policemen. He drew a knife from his pocket and put it to her throat.

"Don't follow me or I'll kill her." He backed out of the drawing room dragging Mary with him across the hall to the front door.

Mr Templeton stood by the door. Lord Chegwidden came out of the drawing room.

"Open the door," demanded Sir Edward.

Lord Chegwidden nodded to Mr Templeton. The door opened and Sir Edward dragged Mary outside.

The only transport was a black police cart and its horse.

Trotting down the drive Mary saw a soldier on a horse. He wore a Hussar's uniform and tasselled hat. Too far away to make out his face Mary wondered and then hoped. The Hussar came close. Now Mary could see it was Johnny.

"Get back," yelled Sir Edward.

The two police officers and Lord Chegwidden stood on the house steps. Johnny dismounted.

"I don't know what the blazes is going on here but, sir, you unhand that young woman or you will join the Russians I sent to Hell!"

Sir Edward pressed the blade against Mary's neck drawing blood from a shallow cut. He had one arm round her neck and held her with her back against his front keeping her off balance.

"If you harm Miss Dunsford, you will hang Sir Edward," Phillips shouted from the steps.

"I'll hang anyway for killing my wife. You will have to catch me first. Now all of you. Stay back." He dragged Mary nearer to the police cart.

To get Mary up the step to the cart, Sir Edward had to loosen his grip on her and reach up to the cart with his knife hand. As soon as he did, Mary grabbed the arm he had around her neck, pulled it tight forward, bent her legs low so that his belly was over her shoulder and then she stood bringing that shoulder up under his pelvis throwing him over her head to land on his back in a move that she had learned many years ago.

Sir Edward dropped his knife. Mary grabbed it, straddled him, and put the knife to his throat.

"No Mary!" shouted Johnny.

She fought back the urge to slash his throat, stood and watched as the police officers dashed forward, handcuffed Sir Edward and roughly threw him in the cart.

"Well Miss Dunsford. I think in due course we shall have your name cleared. I don't know if there will be any charges for you escaping from custody but I shall recommend no further action. By the way, nice move that throw. Where did you learn it?" said Phillips.

Mary looked over at Johnny. "He showed me."

"Are you all right, Mary," cried Lady Eleanor as she dashed down the steps and then threw her arms around her.

"Yes, I'm all right Milady. May I be excused for a moment while I speak to Lieutenant Sandes?"

Lady Eleanor nodded.

Mary took Johnny by the arm and lead him out of earshot of the others, but unbeknown to her, not far enough. "Johnny, I asked a friend to leave a note accepting your proposal of marriage because I wasn't able to. She put it under the wrong tree. I know a lot has happened since you sent me the note and if you want to withdraw the proposal I will understand. You have so much to lose if you marry me."

"Mary, I didn't find your note so I thought you had refused me. I knew that you loved me. And I believed that refusal was not because you were afraid of your identity being discovered but because you knew what would happen to me. I would be disinherited and lose my position in society. All through the war I could only think of you."

"I still love you, Johnny. Now that my identity is known I have nothing to hide. But you will still be disinherited if we marry and that is such a terrible thing for you. I would live happily with you in poverty but I could not let that happen to you."

"We landed at Portsmouth this morning and I came directly here. My intention was to take you with me to Liverpool and board a ship to America where we could be together safe from your identity being compromised. Now that doesn't matter. I shall go to my parents and tell them that I am to marry you and if I am disinherited then so be it. I shall not give up the woman I love."

He threw his arms around her and kissed her gently on the lips.

"Ahem," Mary turned to see Lady Eleanor standing behind her. "This is the young man? I heard what you said, not eavesdropping I can assure you. You were less than discreet in your conversation. I may have the solution."

Epilogue

Lord Chegwidden stood at the drawing room fireplace with his hands behind his back, rocking on his feet. Lady Eleanor sat in her wing backed chair embroidering a napkin. Mary sat next to Johnny on the sofa.

"The solicitor will be here shortly with the paperwork. He located your father and he signed it for a consideration. Are there any questions?" said Lord Chegwidden.

"Are you absolutely sure about this, sir?" said Mary.

"I am. We were not blessed with children," said Lord Chegwidden.

Lady Eleanor smiled. "I am too, Mary. It may be unusual at your age to be adopted but we have found no legal impediment to it."

"So, as my adopted daughter I insist the wedding takes place in our local church with the reception here. Is that acceptable to you, John?" asked Lord Chegwidden.

"It is sir. And my parents too."

+++

If you read this novella to the end, please give an honest review on Amazon. Thank you.

THE END

Printed in Great Britain
by Amazon

40350770R00098